TRUTH RUNNER

OTHER BOOKS IN
THE SON OF ANGELS: JONAH STONE SERIES

Spirit Fighter

Fire Prophet

Shadow Chaser

TRUTH RUNNER

Son of Angels
JONAH STONE

Book 4

JEREL LAW

THOMAS NELSON
Since 1798

NASHVILLE   DALLAS   MEXICO CITY   RIO DE JANEIRO

Published in Nashville, Tennessee, by Tommy Nelson. Tommy Nelson is a registered trademark of Thomas Nelson.

Cover illustration by William Graf, © 2013 by Thomas Nelson.

Tommy Nelson titles may be purchased in bulk for educational, business, fund-raising, or sales promotional use. For information, please e-mail SpecialMarkets@ThomasNelson.com.

Scripture quotations are taken from the Holy Bible, New International Version®, NIV®. Copyright © 1973, 1978, 1984, 2011 by Biblica, Inc.™ Used by permission of Zondervan. All rights reserved worldwide. www.zondervan.com

Library of Congress Cataloging-in-Publication Data

Law, Jerel.
    Truth runner / Jerel Law.
        pages cm. — (Son of angels, Jonah Stone ; book 4)
    Summary: Having left Angel School and moved back to his home town to start high school as a "normal" person, Jonah sees the Fallen attacking his friends without their knowledge and must decide whether to continue forging his own path or remember who he really is, turn back to Elohim, and help.
    ISBN 978-1-4003-2287-9 (pbk.)
    [1. Angels—Fiction. 2. Good and evil—Fiction. 3. Faith—Fiction. 4. Christian life—Fiction.] I. Title.
PZ7.L418365Tru 2013
[Fic]—dc23   2013020908

Printed in the United States of America
HB 01.23.2018

For Luke, who gives his heart freely to everyone he meets—may you always run toward the Truth, bringing many with you along the way.

CONTENTS

CONTENTS

PROLOGUE

Jonah's chest heaved in and out, and he tried desperately to breathe again. He leaned over with his hands on his knees, standing in the alleyway close to the street. He'd had to stop, finally, out of fear that his lungs might collapse under the strain. It hurt to breathe, and his heart was pounding too quickly. After a minute, he could finally stand up straight again, and he used up every ounce of courage he had left to peek around the corner, back from where he had come.

There was nothing there. Only the blackness of the city, the top of the Empire State Building set against the cloud-filled sky with a flashing red beacon at its apex.

But he felt it.

He didn't remember how long he had been running or what had gotten him to this point.

Why am I here? What's chasing me?

There was something there, his mind grasping at memories that were floating away like smoke from a fire. He focused, trying to remember, but it wouldn't come to him, and he didn't have time to think about it now.

It was coming again. He couldn't see anything behind him, but he knew it was growing closer, closing in. That was the one thing he knew that was crystal clear. Whatever was after him was relentless. It wasn't going to give up and wasn't going to stop. It would not give in no matter how hard or fast he fled.

Jonah felt the rain begin to pelt down, stinging him in the forehead. It was cold and growing colder, and his hands shook, but not from the temperature. He was afraid, and he couldn't remember ever being more scared than he was right now.

He pulled the hood of his weathered jacket over his shaggy hair and took off running again.

cℕᴐ

Two familiar beeps from underneath his pillow made him open his eyes, just barely. He lay in a puddle of sweat—or was it drool? His mouth had been hanging open and pressed against his pillow after all.

He groped until he found his phone and pulled it out. The brightness of the screen momentarily blinded him, so he closed one eye and squinted at the e-mail message:

11:46 p.m.

Hey, bro. I hope you are doing okay. Did you get my text from the other day? Don't forget, Dad's birthday is coming up soon. You haven't forgotten to get him a present, have you? Don't answer that.

Things are good on our end. Everyone's back and excited. Missing you, of course, and really wishing you were here with us. But everybody deals with things differently, I suppose. Jeremiah and I need to be here. And you . . . well, I guess you needed something different. Trusting Elohim is in control of all this. Let me hear from you soon, okay? J says hi and that he misses you and that whenever he sees you, he's going to hug you and then beat you up . . . whatever.

~Eliza

PART I

CHOICES

But Jonah ran away from the LORD
and headed for Tarshish.

Jonah 1:3 NIV

ONE

JUST A GAME

Jonah dribbled the basketball across the half-court line, surveying the defense. The ball thudded against the hardwood, but he could barely hear it in the noisy gym. Cheers echoed all around, solely coming from one side of the bleachers. He could hear two words rise above the rest. Shouts of "Peacefield!" mixed with equally loud screams of his name: "Jonah!"

Hearing his name being yelled by the high-pitched voices of high school girls caused a smile to creep across his lips. He had experienced moments like this before—but only in his wildest daydreams.

A loud series of claps from the sidelines drew his eyes. "Come on, Jonah! Let's go!"

Coach Marty was still as round as a basketball and somehow had managed to squeeze his way into the head coaching position for the boys' basketball team at Peacefield High. The boys on the team privately joked that they must have given the job to the guy who shouted the loudest. Coach Marty didn't ever speak in a normal voice—he yelled.

Jonah looked down at the kid guarding him. The kid was crouched down, trying to look intimidating, but he couldn't hide the fear in his eyes as he looked up at Jonah. Jonah wasn't exactly surprised by that—he towered over everyone on the court now, having grown another three inches in the past six months.

Jonah made his move. In a blast of blazing speed, he faked to the right. The boy guarding him jumped. Jonah took advantage, pushing past him. The speed he generated with his first two steps put him inside the three-point line. He was almost a blur. *Control yourself, Jonah.*

A quick scan of the rest of the court let him know that two of his teammates were covered, but the other two were wandering free. Grant Newsome was waving his hands frantically; he was standing right underneath the basket. A pass to him would lead to an easy layup.

Jonah instead turned his eyes to the rim. Another defender had stepped in front of him, but Jonah turned his back and quickly spun away as the helpless boy lunged for what he thought was the basketball, but turned out to be an armful of air.

Ignoring his open teammates, he leaped from just inside the free throw line, trying to remember not to push himself off too high. He had to appear normal—human, like the rest of them. His six-foot-six frame soared through the air, and he finally slammed the ball through the rim with such force that the basket shook, appearing for a second as if it would snap under his force.

Jonah hung on the rim for two seconds longer than he needed to, peering into the stands again, catching glimpses of the fans, who had increased their volume even more now and could barely contain themselves. For the extra swinging, he earned a technical foul from the referee, but he didn't care. It was worth it.

Mercifully, after another two minutes, the game ended. Peacefield High: 103, Ashburn Academy: 54. Jonah's teammates surrounded him in the middle of the court, ignoring the dejected players from the losing team who wandered their way back into the visitors' locker room in a daze. Jonah let himself get caught up in the attention, the slaps on his back, the handshakes, and high fives. A couple of little kids from the stands even came up to ask him for his autograph.

One small boy peered up at him with huge eyes. "Jonah, did you know you scored forty-eight points? And thirty of them were on slam dunks!"

Jonah grinned, reaching down to tousle the boy's hair. "Maybe you can do that one day too, little guy."

He looked back up into the stands, where he spotted two lone figures standing on the top row of bleachers. One had a hulking frame, showing off his bulging muscles. The other was smaller and looked more like a teenager. Both wore metallic armor that glittered underneath the fluorescent lights. The outline of their wings cut sharp lines along the wall behind them.

Jonah could see their faces, and even from center court, he could tell they were the only ones in the gym not cheering. In fact, they didn't appear to be very happy at all.

Another kid tugged at Jonah's sleeve, and slowly he pulled his eyes away from the angels. He listened to the boy sing his praises for a minute, and by the time he glanced back up to the stands again, the angels were gone.

Jonah was one of the last ones to leave the gym. He had been cornered by a group of girls as soon as he walked out of the locker room. They had been so excited to talk to him that he hadn't been able to get a word in or escape to head home. Luckily, someone stepped in to rescue him. Jonah felt a slap on his back, and he turned to find his friend Tariq, wearing his typical hundred-watt smile underneath a massive shock of twisty black hair that his friend had taken to calling a "Middle Eastern afro."

"Another fantastic performance by the great Jonah Stone!"

"Tariq," Jonah said, high-fiving the boy and glancing back over his shoulder as they walked toward the door. "Thanks for rescuing me. I thought I'd never get away."

"Rescuing?" he asked, glaring at Jonah. "Who needs rescuing from pretty girls who want your attention? Are you crazy?"

"Yeah, well . . ."

Tariq waved his hand toward the girls, who were watching Jonah leave in disappointment. "Don't worry," he said to them loudly. "I'll call you soon!"

They left the building and headed to the bike rack where their mountain bikes were chained.

"Just think, next year we'll be able to drive," Jonah said as they fumbled with their bike locks in the dark.

"The only drive I'm thinking about right now is that last one you made on that poor, poor boy guarding you," he said. "Right before you hammered that dunk home!" He stood up and pretended to jam the ball through an imaginary hoop. "That was ridiculous, man!"

Jonah felt his face redden. It was one thing to talk about his play after the game with kids and other people he didn't really know. But Tariq had been his friend since the second grade, and he probably wasn't going to accept Jonah's new basketball skills without asking some questions. "It was okay," Jonah said softly. "Not really all that great when you think about it."

"Seriously, Jonah, you don't mean that. I've watched every one of these last five games, and what you are doing out there is crazy. I don't know what happened to you last year. But you go away to some special school and come back, and you're, like, ten inches taller and all of a sudden, have these mad basketball skills . . ." His voice trailed off as he shook his head. Jonah was starting to feel even more uncomfortable. "It's almost like you're not human or something."

He swallowed as he pulled his bike out of the rack and swung his leg over the bar. They'd already had this conversation before, so Jonah was sticking to his story. "Hey—it's just a growth spurt. I mean, my whole family is tall. And once I grew a little, my balance got better . . . Come on, I'll race you home."

Tariq wasn't one to back down from a challenge, but Jonah knew the discussion wasn't over for good.

There's no way he could know, Jonah thought. *Surely he wouldn't ever suspect who I really am.*

They pedaled the mile and a half home, Jonah having to work hard to back off on his speed and keep his friend in the race. Right at the end, he pretended he was giving it all he had but getting tired, and just as they got to Tariq's driveway, his friend pulled ahead.

"Good race!" Jonah said, breathing heavily.

"Yeah," mumbled Tariq, riding down his driveway. "But next time you want to let me win, make it a little less obvious."

Jonah's mouth hung open, but he didn't say anything as he watched Tariq pull into his garage and shut the automatic door.

He walked his bike two more blocks down Cranberry Street

to his small, white two-level house. A rusting backboard and rim that had seen better days still stood at the end of the driveway.

He wanted to tell his friend the truth. But what was he supposed to say? *Hey, so I'm not totally human. I'm actually one-quarter angel. It's no big deal, really. I just have some special abilities.*

Jonah shook his head. It still sounded crazy enough in Jonah's head. What level of crazy would he achieve if it came out of his mouth?

Two figures stepped out from behind the willow tree in the front yard. Jonah froze, his instincts causing him to reach down to his side, preparing to pull his angelblade. He sighed loudly when he realized who it was.

"Marcus," he said, eyeing the large one. He glanced at the smaller angel. "Henry." Jonah's shoulders sagged, and he continued to push his bike toward the house.

Henry watched Jonah walk past them, placing his hand on Marcus's chest, keeping him from charging forward, as he was prone to do.

"Camilla sent us here. I guess you realize why, don't you, Jonah?" Henry offered in his normal pleasant voice, without a hint of judgment or anger.

Jonah wheeled around. "Look," he said, glaring. "I'm not doing anything wrong. I am keeping all of my gifts under control."

"You are taking advantage," Marcus said, pushing Henry's hand down and taking a step forward. "You're using these powers for . . . for . . . your own amusement and gain!"

Jonah stepped toward the large angel. As tall as Jonah was, his face met the middle of the angel's chest. But he didn't feel like backing down this time. "I'm not hurting anybody, Marcus! And trust me, I'm not doing nearly what I *could* do out there . . ."

"You're drawing unnecessary attention to yourself," countered Henry. "People are beginning to notice."

"And that's a bad thing?" Jonah asked. "What's wrong with me having a little fun? So what if I can do things other kids can't do?" *I deserve it after the year I've been through,* he thought. *Don't you guys get that? Doesn't Elohim understand that?*

"You won't be able to contain yourself!" answered Marcus. "We saw your little game there tonight. You were barely able to hold yourself back. Your pride is going to get you into some serious trouble."

Henry stepped between them before Jonah could respond. "We all know you have been through so much this year. And taking this time in Peacefield, well, it is certainly your choice. We have kept our distance and given you your space. We are here, on behalf of Camilla, to remind you, though, of who you are. Who you really are, Jonah. You're a quarterling. You are gifted for battle, battle in the hidden realm, a key player in the fight between Elohim and Abaddon."

Jonah looked down at his shoes but didn't say anything as Henry continued.

"When your mom was lost, it was awful."

"She was killed, Henry," Jonah erupted. "She wasn't just lost!"

"All of heaven mourned for you and your family," Marcus said, more steady and quiet. "We are just here to make sure you don't forget."

"Well, thanks a lot for coming, guys," Jonah answered, "but I think I'm doing just fine right here in Peacefield. You can tell Camilla that when you go back."

He turned and headed for the front door, letting go of his bike so that it fell in the grass.

"It's okay, Jonah," Henry called out as Jonah stepped onto the porch. "We're here. You're not alone."

Jonah paused for a second but didn't turn around. *Just go away*, he thought. He put his hand on the doorknob and turned the handle.

TWO

TOUGH CONVERSATIONS

Jonah slowly turned the doorknob, trying to make the door open as quietly as possible. He hoped that his father was already in bed. Ever since he had decided to stay in Peacefield and not return to Angel School, Jonah had found himself avoiding his dad. It wasn't a conscious decision as much as something that had begun slowly and now had become normal. Jonah wasn't even sure why.

His dad seemed to oblige him in this, though, by turning in early most nights or staying in his office with the door pulled shut. When they did speak, it was more than likely to be an argument.

He shut the door and tiptoed past his dad's study. He heard some papers rattle and then suddenly stop. Jonah waited for a few seconds in the hallway. No movement inside, no noise. He knew what was happening. His dad was waiting to see if Jonah was going to come in. But he wasn't calling to him. Jonah imagined himself walking into his dad's office and them embracing in a long-overdue hug. Then he pictured them having a massive screaming match, ending with him barricading himself in his room.

Jonah sighed. He knew his dad was hurting too. He'd lost his wife, the love of his life. *But I lost someone important to me too.*

He pushed aside the impulse to go in, and went to his own room, shutting the door behind him.

Falling down on his pillow, he played the game back through his head. He couldn't even keep track of all the fast breaks, layups, and slam dunks he made. But then he thought about what the angels had said. Their voices lingered in his mind, even though he forcibly tried to push the thoughts out. Why should they try to keep him from having some fun and enjoying himself? Hadn't he been through enough this year already? Wasn't it all right to enjoy some popularity for a change? His phone was beeping, and he reached for it, realizing he had nine text messages from different friends at school, congratulating him on the game. He clicked through them slowly, savoring the words, and responded to a few.

But Henry's comments wouldn't leave him alone. *"You're drawing unnecessary attention to yourself. People are beginning to notice."*

He tossed his phone back down on his bed and shifted uncomfortably on his pillow. As much as he tried, he couldn't get away from it. *Why did those angels have to come anyway?*

He grabbed the phone again and opened it up to his photos. Locating the folder marked "Mom," he flipped slowly through the pictures. The family portrait they used for Christmas cards three years ago; a shot of Eleanor and Benjamin, smiling, holding Jonah when he was a baby; one of him and his mom, her arms draped around his neck, at the park. He paused on this one for a while, touching the screen softly with his thumb. It was as close as he could come to touching her now.

He felt the tears well up in his eyes, and he threw the phone back onto the bed and went to take a shower. He wished his mom had seen him play tonight. He wanted to talk to her again, just hear her voice. He wished she were here.

He made the water as hot as he could stand and covered his face with a washcloth, trying to muffle his sobs as he leaned against the tile wall.

✧

"How'd the game go last night?"

His dad was fiddling around in the kitchen, fixing coffee and cereal and opening drawers until he found what he needed. Jonah watched his dad fumble through the kitchen almost every morning, wondering when he would ever figure out where everything was. Mr. Stone finally found a packet of sugar, ripped the top off, and poured the contents into his steaming mug.

"It went okay." Jonah shrugged. "Not that you would know."

It was an open invitation to a fight, and he couldn't resist the barb, even though he felt bad as soon as he said it. His dad eyed him from behind his thick glasses, but pursed his lips and said nothing, suddenly seeming to take great interest in stirring his coffee.

Jonah opened his mouth to say something, perhaps apologize, but then decided against it. He stepped past his father, reaching into the cabinet to grab a granola bar. Snagging a bottle of water from the refrigerator, he mumbled a good-bye, slung his knapsack on his back, and bolted for the door.

"Good morning, Jonah," came a voice from above. Cassandra, the Stone family guardian angel, was sitting in her usual morning spot, perched in the tree in the front yard.

He glanced up at her but kept walking. "You know I'm trying to ignore you, right?"

She smiled, waving to him. "Oh, I've gotten that message, loud and clear."

"Well"—he turned around—"why do you keep bugging me then? Can't you guys see I'm doing just fine?"

Cassandra eyed him thoughtfully. "I just want you to know that I'm not ignoring you."

He waved her off and picked up his bike out of the yard. "I need to go to school. How about not following me, okay?"

Jonah knew he couldn't tell the angels what to do any more than he could tell Elohim what to do, but maybe she would listen today. He pushed off on his bike and pedaled himself into the street.

He was a sophomore at Peacefield High School, but ever since he made the basketball team and had starred in the last five games—all wins—he had been treated like the king of the campus. As soon as he pulled his bike up to the rack and locked it down, a couple of senior guys came over to congratulate him on last night's game. Three girls, all members of the cheerleading squad, scampered over, gushing about it too. He felt his face grow hot and flushed, but he talked to them for a few minutes before he walked into school.

All of the newfound attention made it easy to ignore what he could still see—the things no one else could, the spiritual creatures in the hidden realm. Across the lawn, he saw something small and black clamped onto the back of a tall boy with a downcast face who was walking on the sidewalk. Pulling his eyes away, Jonah tried to forget the image.

But as he walked into the hallway full of students at their lockers loudly milling around, waiting for the morning bell to ring, he couldn't help but see the rest.

There was another fallen angel draped across a girl's shoulders. And one was whispering into a kid's ear as he walked down the hall. Yet another was flying from kid to kid, taunting each in turn. As Jonah approached, the fallen angel locked eyes with him, glaring. And then, grinning wildly, it moved on, continuing to work on the unsuspecting students.

This was the scene Jonah walked into every day now. Once the Fallen realized he wasn't going to do anything, they had become very bold.

Jonah veered off from the crowd and headed to his locker.

"Boy, things sure have changed around here," Tariq said from behind him. Jonah saw his friend watching the junior varsity cheer squad walk down the hall.

"Yeah," Jonah answered, his mind distracted by the flying fallen angel still tormenting kids in the hallway. "I guess so."

"Uh-oh," mumbled Tariq, who was suddenly more interested in his locker than the cheerleaders.

Jonah saw why. Zack Smellman, Carl Fong, and Peter Snodgrass were making a beeline for them, each with identical scowls on their faces. Fong and Snodgrass both grabbed one of Tariq's shoulders and slammed him against his locker, and then held him flat against it.

"I think you and I need to have a little conversation," sneered Zack, right up in Tariq's face, "about how much money you owe me."

"Oww! Let go!" the much smaller Tariq said. "This isn't your school or your hallway! I can do whatever I want—"

"Hi, guys," interrupted Jonah, smiling at the three boys. They seemed to notice him for the first time. The boys immediately let go of Tariq, who rubbed his shoulders. "Is there some kind of problem here that I can help with?"

"Jonah!" Zack said with a sheepish grin. "We didn't see you standing there. I guess we were focused on our friend Tariq here, who owes us some money."

"Friend, huh?" Jonah said, slapping his hand firmly on Zack's arm. "Didn't seem too friendly there, Zack."

"Ha." He laughed, patting Tariq on the arm gently and straightening his shirt for him. "We were just messing around, you know?"

"Yeah, I know," Jonah said, stepping a little closer, towering over them with his lanky frame.

"But you know," Zack said, stuffing his hands into his pockets, "I think we're good with Tariq, don't you, boys?"

His underlings looked at him blankly, confused, but slowly nodded.

"Good game last night," Zack said as they walked away. "Really awesome. Way to go." He smiled again, waved at Jonah and Tariq, and pulled the other two down the hallway with him.

Tariq blinked up at Jonah. "Well, that was . . . different."

Jonah slapped his friend on the back as they began to walk toward their first-period class together. "Welcome to a new day, my friend," he said, smiling. "Now, why exactly do they think you owe them money?"

Jonah listened to Tariq's long-winded explanation as they walked along, something about a booming but not-exactly-in-the-school-rules candy bar selling business, and Zack demanding protection money, threatening to either beat him up or go to the principal if he didn't pay.

Jonah nodded, halfway listening, but with the rest of his mind in a different place. He had passed by no less than four more fallen angels, and each one had given him the same look as the first.

We're killing these kids, and you're not going to do one thing about it...

∽

After Jonah's fifth-period class, he ran by the boys' bathroom. As he was washing his hands, something in the mirror caught his eye and he looked up. To his surprise, his face—and everything else he saw—melted away. In its place, another face came into view.

It was Eliza, with her face drawn up and tight. She looked concerned and like she was searching for something. Jonah reached his hand out to touch the mirror, but then the scene switched. Jeremiah was there now, walking, and alone. He shivered against a chilly wind but kept moving forward. He was searching for something too.

Jonah blinked and saw his own face again.

He glanced around to make sure no one else was watching him. He quickly threw some water on his face, shook his head a couple of times, and hurried back into the hallway.

∽

10:19 p.m.

Hey, Everything's good here. Not too much going on. Don't worry about me. I'm fine. Getting to school on time, doing my homework—you know, all of the stuff you would be worried about. Dad is good, I think. We haven't talked a lot lately. But basketball is awesome—did you see the article in the Peacefield News sports page about me? Hope you guys are okay. Tell little bro hello, and that next time I see him he will get the biggest wedgie of his life.

Later, Jonah

THREE

MOVING TRUCK ESCAPE

The fallen angels were gathering across the street, and doing it quickly. Some were standing, others knelt, and more than a few filled the sky just above. All of them had their bows loaded with arrows, toxic flames burning at the tips.

They were hunting.

Eliza peered around the corner just enough to assess their situation. They had been out to pick up a few essentials, but she wasn't exactly surprised they'd run into trouble. Being out, away from the relative protection of the convent and their school, was always risky. The Fallen were everywhere.

Eliza was only fourteen, but when it came to fights with Abaddon's evil minions, she had more experience than any of the rest of the quarterlings—except Jonah, of course. But he wasn't here. And although it made her uncomfortable at times, when the other kids began to look to her for leadership, she didn't shy away.

She focused on the one who appeared to be leading. His

blackened, gnarled face twisted in anger, shouting unrecognizable commands to his underlings. Eliza had a hard time believing that this crusty-skinned, yellow-eyed creature used to be an angel.

Eliza saw the flaming arrow headed toward her just in time and pulled her head back. It crashed into the concrete wall behind her, disintegrating into dust and falling to the grimy street.

"Again?" she said to herself, quickly raising her arms and producing the shield of faith. It was the first gift she had been given, and she had learned to use it well. It took a simple combination of faith and concentration, and she was the best in Angel School at making it. She'd also received an angelblade last year and was still trying to refine her skills with the helmet of salvation.

"Get over here. Now!" she called out to Jeremiah, who, as usual, was about to charge ahead with no plan. She took two steps forward, causing him to enter the bubble of protection just before another arrow exploded into it, shattering harmlessly. "That one was meant for you, you know."

"Yeah, yeah," Jeremiah muttered. "I think what they need is a dose of the belt of truth."

Eliza grimaced. "I think what you need is not to get killed. It's your fault we're in this mess anyway."

A blond-haired boy on the other side of the alley was shooting arrows as fast as he could, most of them finding their mark into the fallen angels across the street. Frederick had to pull back against the wall, though, as a barrage of enemy arrows hit the wall all around him. He glanced over at Eliza and Jeremiah, behind the safety of the shield.

"I'll cover you, Frederick! Go!" David's voice called out from behind them. Eliza knew that he and Julia had fallen back slightly, and that Julia was probably protecting David with her shield too.

Glimmering white arrows began to whiz past them and toward the charging Fallen.

"Now!" she screamed to Frederick. He didn't need any more encouragement. He crouched as he ran and then dove across the pavement, rolling himself into the protection of her shield of faith. An arrow brushed by his head just as he entered.

"That one was a little too close," he said, picking himself up quickly and preparing to fire again, this time from inside the bubble.

Jeremiah had taken a moment to concentrate and pray and was now standing with his feet apart as the golden belt of truth appeared around his waist. He began to utter truths about Elohim out loud, and each time a blast of white hot light came from the belt.

"Elohim is more powerful than all of you put together!" A blast ripped into the closest fallen one. "Elohim is our rock and strength!" Another one took out two of them at once.

"Good job, Jeremiah!" his sister said, encouraging him. "Keep it going!"

But as he was preparing for the next blast, a mangy dog walked around the corner and right in front of them. The dog's ribs were showing through his shaggy coat, and he looked as if he hadn't eaten in days.

He turned toward the quarterlings and barked. It wasn't the bark that startled Eliza, though. It was his eyes—they were the same sickly yellow as the Fallens'.

"It's time to go, guys," said Frederick, his gaze locked with the dog. Eliza knew he was right. "We're in over our heads."

The sound of barking grew louder, and suddenly a horde of dogs turned the corner. Eliza dropped her shield, grabbed Jeremiah by the shoulder, and began to run. Frederick, Julia, and David did the same, doing their best to stay behind cover as they retreated.

Eliza hoped the alley would lead to another city street, and they could figure out a way to either lose their attackers there or stand their ground. What they saw ahead, though, almost stopped them in their tracks.

A chain-link fence ran between the buildings, less than fifty feet ahead.

"We can climb it or jump it!" Frederick shouted. "Come on!"

"Not all of us can do that!" answered Eliza. She glanced back at the animals, bearing down on them. Then she looked around frantically, noticing several darkened doors leading into the buildings that flanked the alley.

"The doors!" she said. "Inside!"

David was the farthest along and pushed his body against a door to the right. But it was locked.

"Let me at it," said Frederick. Summoning his angel strength, he pushed with everything he had, popping the lock and shoving the door open. Julia and David followed him in.

Eliza turned to head toward the same door when Jeremiah hit the ground.

"Jeremiah!" she yelled, her frustration boiling through as she realized that he had tripped over his shoelaces. She stopped in her tracks, knowing they had only a few precious seconds before the dogs were on them, and then behind them, the fallen angels, who were clearly controlling the street animals. Yanking him up off the ground with one hand, she turned to the nearest door with the other, grabbing the handle and praying all at once.

"Elohim, please open this door!"

She turned the handle, and the rusty door opened. Eliza didn't care where it led to as long as it could give them cover from both of their attackers for a few seconds. They rushed in, and Jeremiah slammed it shut behind them and turned the old dead bolt.

"The others . . . ," said Jeremiah, looking up at Eliza.

"I saw them run into the other door," she answered. "They made it in, so hopefully they're safe."

The dogs slammed against the door, causing both of them to leap backward. It sounded like they were taking turns banging their heads against it while barking as loud as they could.

"I don't think we're going to get out the way we came in," he said, standing up and dusting off his jeans. "Let's figure out where we are."

Eliza glanced around, nodding. "That's fine. But just remember, there weren't just dogs out there. The Fallen were right behind them."

"They were controlling the animals, weren't they?" he asked. "Did you get a look at their eyes?"

"I've seen them do that before," she muttered, thinking back to an encounter she and Jonah had had with a pack of cougars a few years ago. "Trust me, we don't want to be anywhere near those animals."

"This building seems smaller than I thought it would be," Jeremiah said as he looked around the room. They were in a storage space jammed with all kinds of odds and ends—paint cans stacked in the corner, a yellow rolling mop and bucket, a desk covered with a random assortment of hammers, wrenches, screws, and nails, and a couple of desks wedged against the walls and beside each other.

There was another door in front of them. "Let's see where this goes," Jeremiah said, and before she could stop him, he flung the door open.

They suddenly found themselves in a brightly lit factory with assembly lines full of workers filling up an enormous warehouse floor. They were dressed in blue aprons and standing over tables with conveyer belts churning along as they picked and sorted various objects. Most were women, although a few men were there too. Their hands were moving fast as they focused on their work.

When Eliza and Jeremiah entered the room, none of them noticed.

"They're not even looking up at us," Jeremiah said.

"We're still in the hidden realm, remember?" Eliza said. They had entered into that secret, invisible world, where the battle between Abaddon and Elohim takes place, when they realized they would have to fight.

Jeremiah pointed across the expansive room to a set of double doors with a red Exit sign above. "Looks like that's our way out of here."

"Yeah," Eliza said, grabbing his elbow before he had a chance to explore anywhere else. "Come on."

They walked in between two rows of workers, bent over their stations. They were sorting purses of all shapes and sizes that were coming down the moving belts. The bags were being grouped and boxed.

"Stop pulling my arm so hard!" Jeremiah said, jerking his elbow back. "You need to lighten up a little bit here."

"Lighten up?" Eliza asked as she hurried them along, the thought of it impossible at the moment. "You want me to lighten up, after you almost got us killed out there? We were supposed to stay together!"

Jeremiah sighed, but he didn't say anything.

"What is it?" she asked. It was normally impossible to get Jeremiah to be that quiet.

"I thought I saw something, that's all."

She eyed him. "Saw something?"

He cut his eyes toward her. "Well, someone, actually."

Eliza folded her arms as they stood in the middle of the factory floor. "Spit it out. We don't have all day."

"I saw Mom," he said, his lower lip trembling. "I promise you, it was her. She was across the street . . . she waved at me . . . then she walked off, and I . . ."

"Jeremiah," she said softly, placing her arm lightly around his neck. "I'm sure you thought you saw her. There are a lot of people out there on the street, and I can see how someone could look like Mom, but—"

He wrenched himself away from her, glaring. "I know what I saw."

"We don't have time for this right now," she said, frustrated. "Let's just get out of here and find the others. Okay?"

They moved along toward the exit doors ahead. Eliza wanted nothing more at this point than to find the comfort and safety of the convent. But the door cracked open ahead, and light from outside came shining through. In front of the light, a sharp silhouette cut in.

Eliza and Jeremiah could see the outline of wings against the cinder block wall.

"Oh boy," said Eliza.

Jeremiah was already looking around the room. To their right, in the corner of the room, was a set of steps heading down.

"There has to be an exit downstairs too," he said. "Come on!"

He was pulling her now, hopping up onto the conveyor belt.

"Whoa, Jeremiah! Hang on!" she said, trying to keep her balance as they hit the moving belt.

He hopped down on the floor again, then up onto the next one. They crossed two more, moving in between the workers. Most of them continued doing their jobs, their heads down, with no idea what was happening in the hidden realm. Eliza saw one of them, though, a young man, look up right at her, almost like he could see. He reached his hand into the collar of his shirt and pulled out a necklace. He had a disturbed look on his face. On the end of the band was a cross, and he kissed it and closed his eyes, apparently saying a quick prayer. As Eliza jumped past him, she noticed a small tendril of light begin to extend from his body upward.

Good, she thought. *We can use all the prayers we can get.*

They leaped from the last table when the battle cries of the Fallen echoed in the room. The creature was calling to the others to join in the pursuit. Once again, Eliza felt the fear rise. One hit from an arrow and they would be dead.

She glanced back to see a group of them rising up, flying over the clueless workers.

"Get to those steps, Jeremiah!" she cried.

They finally made it to the steps and leaped down them three at a time, and Jeremiah pushed through a metal door. Flaming arrows blasted into the wall just above them, along with a spear for good measure.

It was colder down here, and the fluorescent lights revealed rows and rows of cars. They were in an underground parking lot.

"Let's find the exit and get out of here fast," said Eliza.

"Straight ahead!" Jeremiah said, and they began to run down the middle lane of the lot, toward the large exit sign where the road curved to the right and up.

Their feet slammed against the pavement, pushing along toward the entrance. Just a few more yards and they would be there.

They were almost to the end of the dark lot when a group of fallen angels rounded the corner, down from the street level, directly in front of them. Eliza and Jeremiah screeched to a halt. She could feel the pursuers behind them—they were trapped.

There were at least ten Fallen walking toward them, several with swords drawn, red flames flickering along the blades, licking the air with heat and fire.

"You two have given us quite a chase," the one in front growled. "These city streets can be dangerous. Too bad for you, you ended up on the wrong one."

The others grunted their approval as his eyes gleamed in the dim light. "But there's nowhere to go now, is there?"

Eliza defiantly raised her hands and produced a shield of faith around her and Jeremiah. "Whatever happens," she said, trying to keep her voice from trembling, "we both know who is going to win this battle, don't we?"

Another fallen angel spoke from behind them. "Maybe so, but I also think we know who is going to win this particular fight."

The laughs of the Fallen echoed off the low concrete ceiling. Eliza said a quick prayer to Elohim for support, and her shield grew brighter. She would need all of her strength if they were going to withstand the attack. But she knew that there were too many. After a certain number of arrow blasts her shield would be rendered ineffective. She would grow tired and have to drop her arms. She could pull out her angelblade . . . but they would simply outlast her.

They were done for before they even began fighting.

The faint sound of a motor went unnoticed by the fallen angels. It grew a little louder, but they didn't see the truck until it was rounding the corner behind Eliza and Jeremiah. A yellow moving truck with blank sides, no lettering, pulled toward them. The Fallen behind them had to move quickly to avoid getting run over. They leaped or flew out of the way.

Eliza glanced down at Jeremiah and knew she had no choice but to, at least momentarily, put the shield down.

"Drop the shield right before it gets here, Eliza, and follow me," Jeremiah whispered when their eyes met.

The truck was almost on top of them when she let her hands down. They ran around to its side, allowing it to pass them. The driver, a man with a hat pulled down low, pulled forward, unaware of the battle that was about to take place all around him.

The truck lurched forward, starting to turn upward toward the street. The fallen angels in front had to move out of the way now.

"Now, Eliza!"

He hopped up onto the back bumper of the moving truck, turning toward their enemies behind them.

"Elohim has already won the final battle!" Jeremiah cried.

A blast came from Jeremiah's belt of truth, hitting the first fallen angel and slamming him against the wall before he disintegrated into dust.

He lifted up the handle on the door on the back of the truck and swung it open. It flailed wildly back and forth as the truck rounded the turn, but he was able to hold it open while Eliza dove in. He followed her, slamming the door behind him and landing on top of her in the darkness.

They felt the truck move up, out of the basement lot, and turn left onto a street. Remaining as still as they possibly could, they listened for their attackers.

"You got us out of there, Jeremiah," Eliza said. "But they know where we are now. All they have to do is follow this truck."

FOUR

THE PASSING

Eliza and Jeremiah sat up, leaning against the truck doors, adjusting once again to the darkness.

Out of instinct, Eliza raised her hands and formed a shield of faith to cover them. The soft glow of yellowish white cast a faint light into the back of the van. It was empty, except for a couple of buckets, some brooms, and a stack of cleaning rags.

Jeremiah tugged at his lip. "Do you think she could still be alive?" he blurted out.

Eliza rolled her eyes. "We both saw Mom die, didn't we?" It came out harsher than she had meant it to, and she softened her voice when she saw him hang his head. "I know you'd like to see her again. We all would. But there's no way it was her back there. I'm sorry."

She stroked the back of his head for a few seconds.

"Listen," she said, leaning down and speaking close to his ear. "The next time this truck stops, we need to be prepared to jump out. Okay? I think we've gone far enough that our chances now will be as good as any."

The truck lurched to a stop and began to idle.

"Okay," she said, moving to the back of the truck. "It's time to get off!"

She didn't wait for him to agree. She threw the latch open, and light flooded the bay of the truck. Eliza grabbed Jeremiah's arm, and they jumped down onto the street. She was able to latch the truck door closed just before it began to move again.

A city bus was behind them, and as the stoplight turned green, the driver hit the gas.

"Quick, this way!" They ran to the sidewalk, barely avoiding the front bumper of the enormous bus, and crouched down behind a kiosk full of I Heart NY T-shirts.

"Hey, I wouldn't mind getting a couple of these shirts," Jeremiah said, momentarily distracted. He stood up. "I wonder what size I need?"

"Jeremiah!" she said, dragging him to the ground and pointing her finger in his face. "You listen to me. We are not here to buy T-shirts! That's the wandering attitude that got us in trouble in the first place." She glared at him as meanly as she could. "You are going to do exactly . . . what . . . I . . . say!"

He gulped and nodded. Thankfully for him, Eliza's phone pinged. She climbed off him and reached in her back pocket, studying the text.

"Good," she said. "The others made it back to the convent." She began to type absurdly fast. "The angels will be here soon to escort us home."

"Cool!"

"Yeah," she said, rolling her eyes. "Really cool, Jeremiah."

He thought about it for a few seconds more. "Does this mean we're going to have to have a talk with Camilla now?"

Eliza stuck her finger in his chest. "No," she said, a smile emerging on her face for the first time all morning. "It means that *you* are going to have a talk with Camilla. And Elohim help you . . ."

"Oh."

A group of the Fallen dotted the sky to their left, quickly moving down the street.

"Get down!" Eliza whispered. She watched them from around the edge of the kiosk. They slowed down, looking carefully along both sides of the street. One particularly large fallen angel, with muscles bulging from underneath his black armor, flew along the shops just down the block from them. He looked carefully in each window, searching.

"He's going to see us," Jeremiah said, looking around, trying to figure out what they could do. "Underneath!"

They scrambled to wedge themselves under the cart as fast as they could. Looking out from beneath the cart as the fallen angel hovered by, they held their breath and tried to remain utterly still.

Eliza and Jeremiah were lying on the cold concrete face-to-face. She locked eyes with him and glared, trying to will her squiggly little brother not to move or make a sound and knowing it was almost impossible. She even prayed silently, *Elohim, please let this bad guy pass by, and please, please let Jeremiah be able to be still.* She could tell just by the look on his face that he was having a hard time. He closed his eyes, squinting hard, as if he were trying to hold something in.

She had seen that look before.

Oh no, she thought. Grabbing him by the wrist, she squeezed him just enough for him to know that he needed to hang on.

Peeling one eye over, she saw the feet of the fallen angel suspended in the air, right above them. He wasn't moving. He had paused.

And then, slowly, the foot—the creature—began to move. Away from the cart, farther away from them.

Eliza slowly breathed out. They had made it.

But then a loud squeaking sound erupted right beside her.

She spun her head toward him, but all he could do was raise his eyebrows, unable to hold in a small grin, even in these circumstances.

Now she knew why he appeared to be holding in something. Leave it to her little brother to pass gas at the worst possible moment.

Eliza covered her nose and mouth as the awful smell filtered toward their noses. Her eyes caught movement again outside, though, and her stomach sank.

The fallen angel was back.

She closed her eyes, praying as hard as she could, as she heard him lean down and sniff the air just above them.

He knows we are here. He can smell just as much as I can.

When she opened her eyes again, she found herself looking into a set of yellow orbs attached to a face with an awful, toothy grin, its skin looking as if it had been charred by fire.

But before she could even scream, a silver boot came crashing down on the fallen angel's skull. A blade sliced across the air, and the face turned to ashes.

Quickly, Eliza and Jeremiah pried themselves out from underneath the T-shirt kiosk and found themselves standing in front of a tall female angel.

She sniffed the air too, scrunching up her nose in disgust. "What is that smell?"

∽

Eliza stood outside of Camilla's office back at the Convent of Saint John of the Empty Tomb, which doubled as their quarterling headquarters and home away from home for two years now. It was a shabby old building that no one walking by would take a second look at. Who would be able to tell from the outside that this place housed kids who had angel blood coursing through their veins?

David and Julia stood beside her, all of them quiet, listening to as much of the one-sided conversation as they could hear through the thick closed door.

Eliza squirmed. She wanted Jeremiah to get in trouble for putting them in a dangerous situation, but she couldn't help but feel a little bit sorry for him as she listened to Camilla lecture him.

"And furthermore, young Jeremiah, you are not, under any circumstances, to ever wander away from your group again. Don't you understand how much danger you put your fellow quarterlings in, including your own sister? There are battles going on all over the hidden realm, significant battles between the forces of Elohim and those of Abaddon himself, and we cannot afford to divert troops to go save a group of irresponsible kids who have gotten themselves in over their heads. Is that clear?"

Eliza heard his muffled response.

"Very well, then," she heard Camilla say, her voice softening. "You are a wonderful student here, Jeremiah, with unlimited potential. Please don't do anything that would jeopardize that."

Eliza pulled back as the door opened, and Jeremiah, with sagging shoulders, emerged.

"Well," he said, looking up at them with wide eyes, "sorry I put you all in danger. I'll try not to do it again."

He'd been punished enough. Eliza rolled her eyes and pulled him into a hug.

FIVE

NEW GIFTS

Eliza finally pulled her face up from the deep crease in her pillow, which was now almost soaking wet and smeared with the hint of blue eyeliner she had started to use. She glanced over to see if Julia was here. She hadn't heard the door open, but she also was a little unsure how long she had been crying.

The wave had hit her in the hallway, down with Jeremiah, as she felt the momentary, irrational hope that maybe a phone call home to her mom could comfort her brother. That thought was followed almost immediately, though, with reality hitting her once again out of nowhere—that her mom was dead and there would never be any more phone calls.

Eliza suddenly hated the feeling of having to be the one to comfort Jeremiah. She hated the fact that she had no one to talk to. She wished Jonah were here, and she resented him for staying away. She felt alone.

Half walking, half running to her room, she slammed the door behind her, grateful that Julia had decided to go downstairs to grab a snack. Flopping herself onto her bed, she had buried her face in her pillow, hoping the sobs wouldn't be heard by anyone else. This was the third time this week she had done the same thing.

She was sitting on the edge of her bed, cleaning her glasses with a tissue, when the door to her cramped room opened. Julia, her roommate from Brazil for the last two years, came in holding two steaming mugs.

"I brought you something to drink. Your favorite tea," she said, smiling. She looked closer at Eliza's face. "Are you all right?"

Eliza nodded, rubbing her eyes, pressing her glasses onto her face, and taking the mug. She forced a smile. "Thanks for this. I'm doing fine."

Eliza stood up and looked at her face in the mirror above the sink. She looked puffy and red, and there was no hiding the fact that she'd lost it.

She saw Julia standing behind her in the mirror, blinking and looking as if she was trying to say something but wasn't quite sure how. Finally she just blurted out, "Are you sure? I'm worried about you, Eliza. This isn't the only time I've found you crying and upset this week. It's hard to hide when you've been sobbing, believe me, I know. There are times when I miss my family back in Brazil, and—"

Eliza whirled around, fire in her eyes now, not tears. Julia gulped and immediately backpedaled.

"I'm sorry. I know it's nothing compared to . . . to losing your mom. I can't imagine what you're going through, so the only thing I have to relate it to is, well, missing my family back home."

Eliza's temper flared, but she bit her tongue and told herself to calm down. A year or two ago she wouldn't have been able to control the rising tide of her temper, but Elohim was helping her.

She took a deep breath, and instead of lashing out, reached out to her friend and hugged her. It wasn't the same as having her mom there, but it was nice to have a friend who really cared.

"I know you love me," Eliza whispered, a tear slipping down her cheek again. "Thank you. You're a good friend. It's just . . ."

She knew if she continued, she would be buried in her pillow again.

"It's okay," said Julia, patting Eliza on the back comfortingly. "You're okay. Elohim really cares about you. All of us do."

Eliza nodded, pushed herself away, and grabbed the box of tissues. She then turned toward the mirror once more, with the tall task of making her face look as if she hadn't been sobbing for the past half hour.

When she finally made it downstairs to dinner, long after everyone else had started, she saw a group of kids crowding around Jeremiah, who was telling them in great detail about their adventure earlier. He apparently was relating the part about how he had caused them to be discovered by the fallen angel under the T-shirt cart and was adding in his own sound effects for good measure. The boys were red-faced with laughter, and even the girls were giggling.

She couldn't help but roll her eyes as she prepared a plateful of green lettuce and vegetables at the salad bar in the corner of the dining hall. *Typical*, she thought. *Jeremiah leads us all down the wrong path, and everyone still loves him.* Even Frederick, who had been with them, was standing there laughing.

"Hey, Eliza," Frederick called out. "Jeremiah was telling us about the factory you guys ran through. And how you were jumping over the conveyor belts . . ." He mimicked the balancing act that Jeremiah had shown him while the other kids giggled. "Is that how it went?"

"Well, you sure are one to be joking around about it, considering your life was in danger just as much as mine was today," she said, and sat down at the end of the long table.

Frederick walked over and sat on the table beside her. "Come on, Eliza," he said in his South African accent. "You have to admit, it's kind of funny now."

"No, I really don't," she answered, taking a big bite of her salad.

"You know what your problem is? You're too tightly wound."

She scowled at him as he walked away. *Too tightly wound . . . I'd like to wind you around a telephone pole*, she thought.

It wasn't long until they were off to their Angel School classes for the night. They met at the New York Public Library, and it was the perfect place for them to hone their special quarterling powers. Since it closed at nine o'clock, and the library director was "sympathetic to the cause," as Camilla had explained, the side door was always left open. But to get there, they had to move into the hidden realm and then walk very quietly from the convent under the guard of angels.

That night Eliza walked along with Julia, just behind Jeremiah and some of the other boys. Within the hidden realm, she could see the mark of Elohim inside each of them. As Elohim's followers, there was a bright, steady glow starting in the center of each of their chests and moving out to fill their entire bodies. She had seen it a thousand times now, but it was still somehow the strangest, most beautiful thing she had ever witnessed.

Andre, the huge Russian quarterling, pulled the door open and held it for everyone while his eyes scanned the grounds of the library.

"After you," he said.

They entered the cavernous library and made their way up

the marble staircase to the third floor. Paintings lined the walls, and the ceilings were covered with gold and silver gilding and more artwork. It was no secret that Eliza loved books, and this library was her favorite building in all of New York City.

The reading room was the best part. Thousands and thousands of books lined the shelves, and the soft glow of the table lamps made the room feel calm and peaceful. The ceiling was painted like the sky, and Eliza had spent more than one afternoon here reading everything she could get her hands on.

The quarterlings had been split into three groups for the fall semester. The first group headed to the set of tables in the corner, where a tall, thin angel named Samuel stood smiling at them, with a tall stack of books beside him.

"Greetings, friends!" Samuel said. "Are we ready for a wonderful night of study once again?"

The muscular angel Marcus stood beside redheaded Taryn in the wide-open space in the middle, having pushed the tables against the wall. They greeted their students and didn't waste any time getting started with their lesson in Angelic Defense for the evening.

Eliza and the third group, which included Jeremiah, Andre, Rupert, and Lania, walked into a smaller room just off the reading room.

"Remember, guys," Eliza said. "Hidden realm?"

Andre stopped at the doorway. "I almost forgot."

They bowed their heads to pray and reemerged into the physical world.

The glow of candlelight shimmered in the doorway, and as they walked in, Reverend Kareem Bashir was sitting on a stool against the back wall of the room.

"Hi, my friends!" he said, with a large smile behind his

neatly trimmed black beard. "I hope you are all doing well this evening. We have a lot to cover, so I want you to go ahead and find your seats."

He was the one human who taught them. As a pastor of a church in the city, he was a friend of Sister Patricia from the convent, and she had invited him to instruct them in the ways of the Spiritual Arts. He also had been let in on their secret identities and powers.

Unlike Samuel's class, where there were tables and chairs set up in rows, Kareem preferred his students to sit in a circle so everyone could see one another. He always pointed out that they would often be able to learn just as much from one another as from him.

"Welcome back to another quarter at Angel School. As you know from the readings you've been assigned, and from our work together over the past year, the Spiritual Arts are extremely important, not only in your work to fight the battle against Abaddon and his dark forces, but in your lives in general. As you follow Elohim in this world, you will need to learn to use certain gifts, disciplines, and skills in order to grow in Him and discover the richness of His relationship with you. Now, let me ask you something—what are the special gifts each of you has?"

Jeremiah's hand shot up. "Eliza got a sword!"

She blushed as Kareem nodded. "Yes, she sure did. What else?"

Andre spoke up. "Rupert can produce a really neat shield, and you should see Lania fire arrows. She's amazing."

Kareem smiled. "And what about you?"

He shrugged. "I'm strong."

"Yes, you are," answered Kareem. "And not just human strength. Each of you has angel blood inside you and has been given very rare, very special gifts because of that. But tonight, we're not going to talk about using any of those physical abilities. There are some other gifts you've been given, you see."

They looked at one another. More gifts? Different abilities?

"Like walking on water, maybe?" Jeremiah said, to the laughter of everyone else.

Kareem chuckled. "I think that one is probably saved for Jesus Himself. No, what I am talking about are gifts that are given to every single believer of Elohim on the planet."

Eliza raised her hand. "You mean, spiritual gifts?"

He pointed to her. "Exactly, Eliza!"

"Oh, great," said Rupert, slouching a little more in his seat. English-born Rupert tended to see the negative in everything, but the others seemed a little disappointed too.

Kareem studied them for a second. "I can see that you don't think these are all that big of a deal. Well, I hope tonight's class will change your mind about that."

He held up his well-worn Bible in front of them. "This says that everyone is given at least one of these gifts—a supernatural ability to do something that serves other people, as well as Elohim Himself. There are all kinds of these gifts like encouragement, leadership, fasting, prayer, faith . . . the list goes on."

"But those are things we can all already do," said Eliza. The others were nodding. "I mean, truthfully, I don't see how those are actual gifts."

"You're right, Eliza!" Kareem said, clearly getting excited. "These are abilities everyone can do. But Elohim has decided to give an extra dose of ability in specific areas to certain people."

"Kind of like it's supercharged or something?" Andre suggested.

"Yes, that's probably a good way to put it."

Lania spoke up in her soft voice. "So how do we know what gifts we have then?"

"Well, we don't have a special process for this, like your other abilities," he answered. Eliza remembered back to their first year of Angel School, when Camilla had them read from certain passages in the Bible, which revealed to angels what their quarterling gifts were. She hadn't told any of them exactly what those gifts were, saying only that Elohim would reveal them Himself when He wanted. Eliza was sure that no one had fully discovered all of his or her quarterling abilities yet.

"What we do have, though," he continued, "is each other. Spiritual gifts are best discovered by our close friends observing us and pointing out what they see."

The students looked at one another a bit uncomfortably, sizing each other up, wondering which gifts their friends had been given.

Kareem sat down and pulled his chair a little closer to them. "So," he said, clapping his hands. "Let's talk! Here's the question I want you to answer—when you think about each of your friends here, what is the thing about him or her that comes to mind most?"

"Rupert likes to complain a lot," Andre offered, apparently trying to be helpful.

Some of the kids laughed. Kareem closed his eyes for a second. "No, Andre, that's not what I mean. Let me rephrase the question. When you think of each of your friends, what is a positive impact you see him or her having on you and people around you? Let's start with Rupert, since you brought up his name. Stand up, please."

Rupert sat with his arms crossed, looking back and forth from Kareem to the other students. "Do I really have to?"

Rupert saw that he didn't have a choice and reluctantly stood.

"Okay," Kareem said. "Who would like to go first?"

They sat, staring at Rupert. A minute passed, then another, and one more. Rupert fidgeted, shifting his weight from one foot to the other.

"Well?" he finally erupted.

Eliza cleared her voice. "I have something to share," she said. "Remember that time when Sister Patricia needed help downstairs, in the quarterling lounge, because the bookshelves were an absolute mess, and no one really wanted to do it? Well, you jumped right in and volunteered, which, honestly, surprised me a little. You seemed excited about it, and you got to work and came up with a really cool way to rearrange the room and organize the shelves into different categories. It was kind of neat to see that happen. And it really made the bookshelves a lot easier to manage down there."

The others were nodding, agreeing with her.

Kareem began to smile, leaning forward on his knees again. "So the rest of you recognized this ability in Rupert too, huh?"

He stood up. "Well, let's put this to the test, then." Kareem stood face-to-face with Rupert, his eyes to the ceiling, thinking. He snapped his fingers. "Okay, I've got it. I'm going to give you a real-life situation of mine that I do need help with. Now, while I ask Rupert for his help, here's what I want from the rest of you. Enter back into the hidden realm and make any observations you can. I have a suspicion that something interesting might occur."

Pop, pop, pop.

One by one, as they bowed their heads and prayed, they disappeared from Kareem's view. He turned his attention back to Rupert, taking his phone out of his pocket and holding it up.

Rupert was still standing with arms folded, not at all enjoying the attention he was getting, but he did seem intrigued.

"Okay, Rupert, here's my situation," their instructor said, glancing at his phone and thumbing through the screen. "The truth is, I am a terrible organizer of my time. I constantly over-book myself, commit to too many things, and I end up missing appointments and making people mad . . ."

Eliza was a little surprised to hear him talk so openly about his disorganized life, but he continued on, explaining in great detail what next week looked like and how he had overbooked himself yet again. She studied the two intently but saw nothing out of the ordinary, even in the hidden realm. Rupert, whose smirk was gone and was now listening, grabbed Kareem's phone in his hand to have a look at the entangled schedule himself.

He looked up at Kareem and smiled. "This isn't that hard to figure out, you know," he said. He leaned over and began to point at the screen, growing more and more excited as he explained how their instructor could solve his scheduling problems.

"Would you look at that," Andre muttered.

"Whoa," Eliza said.

Jeremiah's mouth hung open. "Ooooh."

The same tendrils of white light that were visible in the hidden realm when someone prayed, that usually stretched upward, had begun moving out from Rupert. It started as a barely visible fog, but grew clearer and more defined as he continued speaking. The fingers of light moved toward Kareem, playfully surrounding him, and then moved into his chest.

As they did, Kareem's inner light actually grew just a little bit brighter.

"That is so cool," Eliza exclaimed. Discovering anything for the first time excited her, and she began to speak more rapidly. "He's helping Reverend Bashir by using his spiritual gift, and it is literally making him glow brighter! It's like Elohim is actually involved in it too."

"I know," Lania said. "Isn't it awesome that it's making the one he's helping grow brighter? Not just Rupert alone? I wouldn't have thought it worked that way."

Eliza couldn't wait to share what they were seeing with their instructor and Rupert. They reemerged from the hidden realm as Rupert was telling Kareem about an app he could get on his phone that would help him.

"It's called Org for Dimwits, and it is a fantastic application that will let you input your entire calendar, set up meetings in different categories depending on who you are meeting with, and—"

"Don't you guys want to know what we saw?" Eliza interrupted.

Rupert scowled at the interruption. "Well, sure, I guess."

She explained in detail the tendrils of light and how they were filling Kareem up as Rupert shared his gift.

Kareem stood, smiling, as he heard the excitement in her voice. When she was done, he had them sit down again.

"So does anyone want to take a guess as to what gift you think Rupert has?" he asked.

"The gift of telling people what to do?" Jeremiah asked, raising one eyebrow questioningly.

Kareem laughed. "Well, close, but not exactly."

Eliza raised her hand high. "From the readings we've done and what I have seen in the Bible, I would say administration— the ability to come up with systems and structures that help things work better. It's a pretty phenomenal gift, if you ask me."

He nodded. "And it's pretty cool, isn't it, that they are for

helping each other, not just something that is for our own bene-
fit? What we'll be doing over the next few weeks is discovering
more about each of your gifts, how to use them, and how powerful they can be as we serve Elohim and battle Abaddon. Let me
leave you with one thing tonight: you each have some pretty
amazing physical abilities, but don't underestimate the power of
a spiritual gift. You never know when Elohim might want to use
it in a mighty way."

Everyone wanted to know what his or her own gift was, but it
was time to move on to the next class.

Eliza thought about Jonah as she slid back into the hidden
realm for her next class. What was his spiritual gift? More impor-
tantly, was he okay?

She bowed her head and said a quick prayer for his safety and
strength. She couldn't help but think that he was awfully alone.

1:14 a.m.

Hey Jonah,

*I hope you're doing okay . . . are you lonely? There's no one around you like YOU,
if you know what I mean.*

*We had a great class tonight with Kareem. You would have liked it. Rupert discov-
ered a pretty cool spiritual gift he had no idea he had! And Jeremiah . . . well, don't
even get me started.*

*I miss Mom. I miss you too and wish you were here with us. Give Dad a hug for
me. And tell him I miss him too.*

Love, E

SIX

CRAZINESS
IN THE CAFETERIA

Jonah walked into the Peacefield High cafeteria, his backpack hanging from his shoulder and his new pink socks pulled to just under his knees. He glanced down at them uncertainly, even now. His dad had stared at them at breakfast this morning, giving them a one-word response: "Really?" Jonah had simply shrugged, and that had been the end of that conversation.

Pink socks weren't really his thing, but half of his friends on the basketball team were wearing the same ones. It was in, and so he had sucked it up and shelled out fifteen bucks for them at the sports shop last night.

"Nice socks, Jonah," one of the cheerleaders said, smiling as she walked by. "Those are so cute!"

He was growing used to more attention, so he looked back at her with a smile and said thanks.

The high school cafeteria was so much bigger than the one

back at Granger Community School. It made for a loud, chaotic room that the lunch monitors could barely keep under control.

Jonah walked over to the food line and stared down at the offerings, none of which looked entirely appealing. He sighed, wondering what Eliza and the other quarterlings were having right now. He had a mini-daydream while standing in line of an enormous plate piled high with steaming fried chicken, corn on the cob, mashed potatoes, and gravy—all prepared by nuns who could really cook.

As he watched the lunch lady with the black hairnet slop a cold, gooey substance onto a tray of a kid in front of him, he snapped back into reality.

"Serve you, son?" she called out to him with a scowl on her face. "Hurry along, now, pick something."

"Oh boy," Jonah muttered to himself, finally pointing to the least radioactive-looking tray of food in the buffet line and cringing.

He turned to look for the table where his friends would be, standing still and scanning the entire room for a few seconds. The cafeteria was always divided into sections, but not by the teachers or by room dividers or anything like that. The students separated out into groups themselves, and any kid with even the lowest level of observation skills could easily figure out who they were.

The band kids were in the far corner, not wanting to draw attention to themselves. Beside them, several tables of students dressed mostly in black sat, sullen and mostly quiet. *The goths*, Jonah said to himself. A few were looking over at the band people with scorn. One student kept lobbing balled-up paper napkins at them and laughing.

In the other corner were the students Jonah had been hanging out with—the jocks. They were the loudest, most obnoxious group in the cafeteria. Mostly this section was made up of football and basketball players, with a few baseball players thrown in, as well as the entire cheerleading squad. Mr. Sherman, one of the lunch monitors, stood against the wall near them, his arms crossed.

Although Jonah still tried to ignore it, he couldn't help but see what was happening in the spiritual world too. As he held his tray carefully and walked toward the jock tables, he saw a dozen or more fallen angels hovering over the kids, bouncing back and forth, whispering in ears, standing on tables, digging into their backs, and basically encouraging them to pick on other kids.

"Hey, Darnell," Jonah said, sitting down beside the pencil-thin kid with the blank stare. He hadn't known any of them for very long, and he was still trying to figure out how to fit in. "How's it going?"

"Unnngh," Darnell replied, his mouth stuffed full. Tony was busy listening to a group of ninth-grade boys tell him how great he was and nodding his approval. Mike had his long leg stretched across the floor to the table beside him, his foot wrapped around a chair. When a kid joined his friends with a full lunch tray and tried to sit down, Mike pulled the chair out quickly. The boy ended up flat on his back, with food all over his chest. This sent the three of them into a fit of snorting laughter and high fives.

"That wasn't all that nice," Jonah said, but not loud enough for anyone to hear. These weren't the kids he would have hung out with last year. But he was an athlete now. This was where he belonged. He held up a spoonful of the mystery vegetable on his plate, trying to draw their attention away from the poor kid on the floor. "How about this food? Any guesses as to what this is?"

But none of them were listening. Occasionally a fallen angel would fly by, bend over, and whisper something into their ears. One particularly small, creepy one landed on Darnell's shoulder, glaring at Jonah with a wicked smile as he spoke into the boy's ear. Jonah held his spoon in front of his face for a minute, mesmerized by the fallen creature.

"Why are you staring at me, dude?" Darnell said, looking up at him for the first time. "You look weird."

Jonah blinked a couple of times and shook his head. "Oh, sorry," he stammered. "I was just . . . thinking about something and lost my train of thought."

"Lost your train of thought, did you, Jonah?" the fallen angel squealed, laughing hysterically. "Sure you did! Sure you did!"

Jonah opened his mouth but caught himself before he responded to the creature's taunt.

The basketball player stared back at him, a dull look on his face. "Yeah?"

Jonah forced a smile again. "Nothing, nothing, I was just . . . never mind." He stuffed a spoonful of the goo in his mouth before he could say something that he might regret later.

He felt someone behind him, and then a lunch bag plopped down to his left. The four basketball players looked up in unison but still stared blankly.

"Hi there, everyone!" Amber said as she sat down. She was one of the varsity cheerleaders. The boys all watched as she flipped her long, blond curls behind her shoulder and pulled up a chair close to Jonah. "Do you mind if I sit here, Jonah?"

He stared at her until he realized he probably had the same glazed look as his buddies. He reminded himself that this was one of the perks of sitting at the athlete table. "No, great. That's fine."

She smiled, slid into her chair, and studied Jonah for a few seconds. He swallowed hard, knowing that one of the prettiest girls in school was sitting inches away. The others continued to stare at her too, finally uninterested in their lunches or picking on other kids. Apparently, though, she had eyes for only Jonah.

"I wanted to tell you, in person, how incredible that game was last night," she said as she unwrapped her sandwich and took a small bite. "I mean, the way you took charge of the game, made those other players look like they were just . . . standing still!" She began to laugh, tilting her head back as if it were the funniest thing she could imagine. "I can still see the looks on those poor boys' faces . . ."

Amber continued chattering away about the game, how impressive Jonah was, and how many dunks did he have? Fifteen? And how many points did he score? And did he happen to catch the halftime dance number by the cheerleaders?

Jonah simply nodded his head, interjecting a "yeah" or a "uh-huh" or a "thanks" every so often. But something across the room caught his attention, and he found himself cutting his eyes away from her.

Three groups of fallen angels were forming. One over the band kids, another above the goths, and a third over the top of the jocks. For the first time, it hit him—there were different teams of the Fallen, assigned to the cliques in the school.

Or maybe the Fallen had created the cliques . . .

"Jonah?" Amber said, losing her smile and wrinkling her forehead. "Are you listening to me? I was asking you how you liked the choreography I came up with for the . . ."

He zoned out again, too distracted. The fallen angels were hissing and snarling at the others in the different groups in a language he couldn't understand, but it seemed as if they were hurling insults at each other.

Suddenly, a spitball flew across the cafeteria, hitting a football player named Will Rivera right in the back of his head.

"That's not going to be good," Jonah said, standing slowly.

Amber looked at him strangely, her head cocked sideways. "You don't think the dance moves I came up with were good?"

He ignored her as he watched Will stand slowly—all three hundred and three pounds of him. Will had been named all-conference offensive lineman of the year for three years running. Recruited heavily by Ohio State, Florida, and every other top football school in the United States, he was probably last on anyone's list of people they'd want to meet in a dark alley. Or a cafeteria lunchroom.

"I want to know who did that, and I want to know right now," he said with an eerie calm in his voice. The cafeteria hushed as everyone turned to look at Will, but Jonah saw something no one else could. Perched atop Will's shoulder was a fallen angel, whispering steadily.

No less than six fingers pointed at the same person—a kid wearing all black with his hair hanging into his face. Apparently, his friends weren't the most loyal bunch around.

The kid dressed in black stood up. He wore gloves with the fingers cut out and held his hands out wide.

"I'm sorry," he said, sarcasm in full effect. "Did I hit *you* with that spitball?" He pointed to the girl sitting beside the football player. "'Cause I was aiming for your girlfriend."

Two fallen angels swooped in, at his right and left shoulders, leaning into both of his ears. Jonah's eyes were locked on them, until he saw a swarm of others, floating in the air above the scene.

They were jeering and calling out to the other kids, who by now had turned their full attention to the showdown that was brewing.

Will took off his jacket, placed it on his chair, and took a couple of steps toward the boy. "Are you sure you didn't mean to say, 'I'm sorry, Will. It will never happen again'?"

"Fight!" someone yelled from the back of the room. Jonah saw a glimmer in the kid's eyes as he listened. Soon, the rest of the kids around him were chanting the same word, over and over. "Fight, fight, fight, fight . . ."

Jonah looked for Mr. Sherman, but for some reason, he wasn't at his usual post along the wall. Everyone at the surrounding tables stood up along with Jonah to see what was happening.

The boys were staring each other down, inching closer to one another as the frenzied chanting grew louder. Jonah had seen this happen before, but never so clearly in the invisible world. When kids were together, sometimes the gang mentality came out, and it never ended well.

If only they could see what I see, Jonah thought. *Then they'd really know what was going on.* He watched as the fallen angels swirled around them, faster and faster, intoxicated by the prospect of a fight. They were egging the boys on, whispering who-knew-what into their ears, whatever they could say that would bring about the most destruction possible.

And Jonah was just standing there with the rest of them. Watching.

The kids formed a tight circle around the two boys, and Jonah saw the glint of fury in Will's eyes and his fists clinch. He was about to lose it, and neither Mr. Sherman nor anyone else could stop him now.

Except for . . .

The goth kid was still taunting the football player when Will lowered his head like a bull and charged.

But just as the boys were about to crash into each other, Jonah stepped between them and threw out his arms, keeping them both apart. He was using just enough of his angel strength to stop them from clobbering each other. He glanced upward at the fallen angels, who were now congregating right over him, seething in contempt, now screaming his name.

"Jonah! Jonah Stone! How dare you, Jonah! How dare you!"

"Shut up!" he said, finally boiling over. The goth kid squinted his eyes at Jonah, glancing upward too. "Who exactly are you looking at?"

He ignored the comment. "You two don't need to do this," he said. "It's totally not worth it, trust me."

"Mind your own business, dude," Will said, grabbing Jonah's hand and trying to push it away. He pressed against it but couldn't move it. "Huh?" He looked confused.

"Seriously, guys," Jonah pleaded, looking toward the door. "Mr. Sherman's going to be back in here any minute, you're going to the principal's office, and nothing good is going to come out of this."

The skinny kid tried to push himself away, but Jonah grabbed his arm in a steel grip.

"He hit me with a spitball!" Will said, growing more furious by the second, struggling against Jonah's hold. "He's not gonna get away with that!"

"What are you gonna do about it, meathead?" the boy answered, pushing against Jonah as the fallen angels swirled wildly again. The students were still chanting.

"Calm down, everybody!" Jonah shouted. The two kids were

still straining against him, and he knew he could hold them for a long time. He just didn't know exactly what to do with them now that he was holding them.

"What's going on in here?!" the voice of Mr. Sherman boomed across the room as he came running over. "I leave the cafeteria for one minute to take care of a situation, and then this happens? What's wrong with you kids? Get back to your tables, now!" He broke through their circle and stood with his hands on his hips, glaring at the three boys. The kid in black held his hands up as if he were being arrested, smirking, and backed away, finally turning and hurrying through the door.

"That kid hit me with a spitball, Mr. Sherman!" Will said.

"So you were going to fight him for that and risk getting expelled?" the monitor said. "Sit down, son!"

Will turned back to the football player table but looked back at Jonah, rubbing his hand.

"Stone, you should be playing football, not basketball. No one's been able to hold me back like that before." Will shook his head, bewildered, and buried himself in his lunch tray full of food again.

Jonah took a deep breath, feeling the stares of the students and the glaring watch of Mr. Sherman. Jonah excused himself and walked out into the hallway. He needed to get out of there for a few minutes and regroup.

"You!"

The screech filled his ears as the fallen angel swooped down in front of him. His face was filled with hate and anger, and Jonah couldn't help but take a few steps backward.

"How dare you interfere with our school!"

Jonah glanced around the hallway. There was a girl walking

the opposite direction, but no one else was around. He found himself against a bulletin board along the wall.

"This isn't your school, you know," Jonah answered, looking the fallen one plainly in his yellow eyes. He then looked him over up and down. "And aren't you kind of small to be so bossy, anyway?"

The fallen angel was short and round, and when he heard Jonah's taunt, he looked as if he were going to explode, spinning himself around in a circle before he drew back even closer to Jonah's face.

"You don't know who you're speaking with, do you?" he said, giving Jonah his most threatening stare.

Jonah was unfazed. "I don't really care who you are. I saw what you were doing back there. Pitting the goths against the athletes. Don't think I don't know what you were up to."

He pointed a crusty black finger toward Jonah's eye. "I am Valack, and you will speak to me with respect! I know who you are." He smiled wickedly. "We are all aware, my friends and I, that we have a . . . special creature here with us. But just so you know, this is still our school. It's *my* school. So mind your own business and go back to doing just what you were doing. *Nothing*. And my associates and I will return to what we were doing, and doing so well. Is that understood?"

Jonah sighed. He knew that if he entered the hidden realm, he could take this little guy out with one swipe of his angelblade. A year ago he wouldn't have thought twice about it. But a lot had happened since then. He had jumped up in the middle of that fight, more out of instinct than anything else. But now that he thought about it, he reminded himself that he didn't want to be that guy anymore.

"Fine, fine," Jonah said, looking down at the floor. "Whatever, Valack. Just get out of my face, okay?"

Valack floated in front of him for a minute more, trying to make his point stick. Finally, he backed away, turned, and disappeared around a corner.

Jonah shook his head and started to head for his locker, when a voice called out from behind him.

"Yo, man, what was that all about?"

Jonah turned to see his friend Tariq edging toward him from the cafeteria. Jonah tried to smile, wondering exactly what he had seen.

"I just didn't want to see that kid get broken in half, you know?" he answered, hoping Tariq was talking about him breaking up the fight.

"No, that's not what I'm talking about," Tariq said, folding his arms in front of him. "I'm talking about you, by yourself in the hallway, talking to . . . no one. And did you say . . . Valack, or something?"

Jonah blinked at his friend, wondering if he could play it off. "I don't know what you mean."

"Dude." Tariq stepped up beside him, looking him over carefully. "Are you okay? Do you need to . . . I don't know . . . go see the school psychologist maybe?"

Jonah forced a laugh. "No, of course not. I'm fine. I was just talking to myself."

He knew his friend wasn't buying it. "They make medicine for this kind of thing, you know."

Jonah slapped his friend on the shoulder, trying to come up with any reason he could to leave. "I need to get to my locker and get ready for gym class next period. Seriously," he called out, taking three long steps away and down a different hallway, "I'm okay, all right?"

He turned and waved back to Tariq, just to show that he was, indeed, fine.

"Okay," answered Tariq. He pointed the other direction. "But gym class is that way . . ."

SEVEN

PINNED DOWN

Jonah was definitely feeling a little dazed from the incident in the cafeteria and his conversation with the fallen angel Valack, not to mention the fact that Tariq had clearly overheard him talking in the hallway. He imagined what he must have looked like to his friend. Leaning against the wall, looking up into the air, and talking to no one.

"No wonder he thinks I'm crazy," Jonah muttered to himself. "*I* think I'm crazy, actually."

Who in their right mind spoke to invisible creatures? He just wanted to live a normal, fun, mindless teenage life. He wanted to enjoy being on the basketball team, his friends, not to mention the girls . . . all without the trouble of knowing what was going on behind the scenes.

Why can't I just go back in time, to life before this all happened? Why can't I just forget about things, pretend none of this is real?

He didn't need the stress. He didn't want to be that guy in the cafeteria, the one breaking up fights, the one having to always know more than the rest. The one who could see things no one else could see. The one who lost his mom to bad guys invisible to everyone but him.

He would redouble his efforts. He told himself that no matter what happened the rest of the day, he would ignore what he saw.

Carlton Humphries entered the gymnasium right in front of him.

"Hi, Jonah," he said, waving as he plodded along.

"Hey, Carlton," replied Jonah. Jonah had known Carlton since kindergarten—at least, that's what his mom had always told him. He didn't remember much about it, but apparently they had spent a lot of time together on the playground back then.

They walked into the locker room to change into their required gym clothes. Jonah used to hate this part of his school routine, but since he'd made the basketball team, he didn't mind it so much. Before, it always seemed that some creative form of humiliation was right around the corner—head dunk in the toilet, anyone?—but now, the locker room felt like a second home.

He set his backpack down on a bench in front of a row of empty lockers and pulled out his gym shorts and shirt and began to change. Carlton had walked past him, down toward the corner, but not before Carl Fong began to trail behind him, mimicking his every step, as a couple of other kids howled with laughter. Jonah cut his eyes upward in time to see a fallen angel swoop in, gleeful at the fun these kids were having at Carlton's expense.

Ignore it, Jonah. Remember—it's not worth it.

He grimaced as he saw Carlton's hefty shoulders sag. But Jonah dutifully pulled his eyes away, focusing on the shoe he was untying.

"Hey, look, Carlton's got on his short shorts again!" One of the boys beside Fong was pointing and laughing as Carlton pulled up his shorts. Again, the others sniggered loudly, not even caring that he could hear them.

Jonah glanced at them. They were a little on the short side. *Carlton, why did you have to wear such short shorts? You're not making it any easier for yourself, you know.*

Carlton turned toward the boys. "Shut up!"

This only made them laugh harder. "Oooh, Carlton's getting angry," Fong said. "You guys better watch out!"

Jonah could feel the fallen angels in the room without even having to look. He knew what they were doing—taunting, encouraging the mean kids, and whispering awful things to Carlton, no doubt.

Thankfully, the physical education teacher, Mrs. Schaumburg, came in just then. "Let's go, boys. You're wasting time in there!"

Carlton hurried past the boys and looked at Jonah as he walked by.

A fallen angel glared at Jonah as he flew behind Carlton. "You mind your own business!"

Jonah slammed his locker shut and stared at the ground for a minute, trying to collect his thoughts.

"You coming, Stone?" one of the other basketball players asked.

Jonah looked up. "Yeah, yeah, I'm coming. Right behind you."

Mrs. Schaumburg was a thin, wiry German woman with a thick accent who had apparently been in the military for twenty years before joining Peacefield High as a physical education teacher. That was the rumor, anyway. Jonah believed it. She ran the class like her own private military brigade. She made them do things like jog outside with twenty-five-pound rucksacks on their backs. Or army crawl along the ground underneath a low-hanging blanket of barbed wire she had constructed herself. And she made anyone who complained do fifty push-ups in front of everyone.

Jonah remembered the possibility of those push-ups and hurried across the gym floor to catch up with the others. They were standing in a line against the wall as Mrs. Schaumburg paced in front of them. She eyed him as he joined the line but said nothing. He was safe, for now.

Behind her was a large, square mat.

Stone-faced, she watched them carefully as she spoke. As far as Jonah could remember, he'd never seen her smile. "All right, students. Today we will be testing our skills in a sport as old as the ancient Greeks themselves. It will test your strength, agility, and focus. Wrestling!" She held her hand back toward the mat.

Fong and his friends began high-fiving each other. Carlton, standing beside Jonah, pressed himself even closer to the concrete wall, as if he were hoping to fall through it and disappear from sight.

"I will be instructing you in your technique," she announced, hands on her hips. She glanced at Fong, who was pretending to do a pile driver on an imaginary victim. "Some of you have been watching wrestling on the television. I can assure you, that type of ridiculous behavior has little or nothing to do with the real sport of wrestling we practiced back in my homeland. I was high school champion."

One of the girls tentatively raised her hand. "They had a girls' wrestling team?"

"No!" she said, with the closest thing to a smile on her face Jonah had seen. "Boys. Fifty-kilogram division."

"Oh," the girl said, sinking back with her friends. Then she said again, a little too hopefully, "So only the boys are going to wrestle then?"

"The girls will wrestle the girls, and the boys will wrestle the boys, of course," she said to a new round of ughs. "Now, I need a volunteer to help me demonstrate some moves."

If they all could have taken a step backward, Jonah figured they would have. Everyone grew perfectly still, no one wanting to have to face the absurdity of wrestling with Mrs. Schaumburg.

Jonah suddenly saw a fallen angel drift down from the rafters, land on her shoulder, and whisper something in her ear. She looked directly at Carlton.

"Mr. Humphries," she called out. "Thank you for volunteering. Please step forward."

He blinked from behind his thick-framed glasses. "But . . . I didn't . . . I . . ."

"*Please step over here,*" she insisted, pointing behind her to the blue wrestling mat. "*Now!*"

Carlton staggered forward. The rest of the class snickered, whispering and giggling. Even the girls were now standing up attentively.

Jonah thought for a brief second about volunteering to take his place. It would be the nice thing to do. And with his angel strength, he would certainly have no problem handling Mrs. Schaumburg, let alone anyone else in the class.

Remember, you said you weren't going to get involved?

He stayed put and kept his mouth shut.

Carlton tripped over the edge of the mat and stumbled, barely catching himself before falling on his face. Jonah couldn't imagine a more humiliating scene for Carlton.

Mrs. Schaumburg proceeded to put him through a series

of wrestling moves that, with each one, increased the howling laughter from the kids.

First, he was down on all fours, with Mrs. Schaumburg crouching behind him. He looked up helplessly at Jonah, right before she pulled one of his arms out from under him, flipped him over, and held his leg up in the air while her knee was on his chest.

"Pin!" she called out, slapping the mat twice. The students applauded, egging her on. Jonah was one of the few who didn't clap.

"Get up, Mr. Humphries!" He half leaned, half stood in front of her, glancing at the door, as if he were thinking about making a run for it.

With him standing in front of her, she grabbed him behind the head and quickly flipped him around.

"Come on, Mr. Humphries. Give me some fight!" she said. Clearly, she was getting into it. Suddenly, Carlton was on his back, having been thrown down over her leg. He groaned in pain, closing his eyes tight. She flopped down on top of him, pressing all the air out of his stomach with a *whoosh*.

"Pin!" she exclaimed again, slapping the floor.

"Oooooof," was all Carlton could say.

Jonah watched the fallen angels flittering among the students, encouraging the jeering and laughing.

This is what they do. This is why high school is hard. They drive people away from each other. They isolate people.

After one more wrestling maneuver ended with Carlton gasping for breath on the mat, and Mrs. Schaumburg yelling "Pin!" and slapping the floor, mercifully the demonstration was over. It was time for the rest of them to try their hand.

She numbered them off and paired them together, boys with boys and girls with girls. Jonah ended up with Drake Drummond, one of Fong's cronies, a wispy kid with spiky hair and a permanent smirk.

Jonah was already disgusted with the whole scene today. It might actually be nice to get some aggression out on the mat.

Control yourself, Jonah. You don't want to send this kid to the hospital.

And, of course, since things for kids like Carlton seemed to always work that way, Carlton was paired with Fong.

Two by two, they were called onto the mat, as Mrs. Schaumburg barked out instructions.

"Let's go, Stone," Drake said, within earshot of the other kids. "Let's see what you got."

Jonah smiled at him. "Just remember, you asked for it, Drummond."

He toyed with the boy for a few minutes, letting him appear to have gained the upper hand. Drake stood behind him, holding Jonah's arm behind his back. "You want any more, Stone? Crying for mercy yet?"

Jonah rolled his eyes and, in a flash, spun, reversing the position so that he was now behind the bewildered boy. He hoisted him with one arm onto his shoulder and began spinning.

"This is not what I am talking about!" Mrs. Schaumburg cried. "We are not doing zee professional wrestling moves! Not in here! Put him down, pleaze!"

Jonah shrugged his shoulder. "Okay, Mrs. Schaumburg. If you say so."

He dropped Drake onto the mat and pinned him by lying on Drake's chest, putting his hands behind his head, and staring up at the ceiling. The teacher hopped down on both knees and slapped the mat twice. "Pin!" she shouted.

A smattering of applause came from his classmates. He pretended to tip his hat to them and took his place back against the wall.

"Okay," she said, "who hasn't participated yet?"

"We haven't, Mrs. Schaumburg," Fong said all too happily.

"But I . . . I already . . . ," Carlton began to protest, but she shook her head and beckoned him onto the mat.

Carlton sighed again as Fong grabbed him by the elbow and dragged him out to the middle of the floor.

Carlton stood limply, ready to take his medicine and get it over with. Fong, however, was clearly going to milk the situation for all it was worth. Jonah watched from the wall with the others as they cheered for Fong and threw taunts out at Carlton—all of which somehow went unnoticed by Mrs. Schaumburg.

The fallen angels were swarming around the two boys on the mat as well as the kids along the wall. Jonah knew that every student was able to make their own decisions about the things they said—it wasn't as if they were being controlled by the evil creatures—but the suggestions in their ears certainly didn't help. Without being in the hidden realm, Jonah couldn't tell who had given their lives over to Elohim and could claim His protection. Angels certainly were nowhere in sight.

"Okay, Carlton, don't worry. I'll take it easy on you," Fong said, his eyes twinkling. Fong was short but built like a tree stump, thick, burly, and low to the ground.

Carlton was a good sport, and Jonah was impressed that he even walked out onto the mat and got down in the crouched wrestling position to face Fong. But it was a complete mismatch from the beginning. Fong wasted no time putting Carlton on his back, grinning at all the other kids as Mrs. Schaumburg counted Carlton out.

Jonah felt the urge to run out and help Carlton, but each time it bubbled to the surface, he shoved it away, reminding himself that he wasn't going to get involved. A couple of times he felt so bad for his old friend that he had to look away. When he did look back, he began to watch the fallen angels, as Fong continued to embarrass Carlton. They were practically foaming at the mouth, and the students were following suit.

Finally, after Carlton was pinned for the last time, Mrs. Schaumburg slapped the floor twice and excused the boys back to the wall.

"Tomorrow we will repeat this exercise," she said, as if there was nothing she thought would thrill the students more. With that, she sent them to the locker rooms to get dressed.

Jonah watched as the kids practically sprinted across the gym floor, laughing while glancing back at Carlton. Fong was in the middle, yukking it up the loudest. Carlton hurried past Jonah, his head hanging down, just another day in a long string of humiliating ones for him.

"I'm sorry, Carlton," Jonah called out to him as he passed. "I ... I wish I had ..."

He couldn't finish his sentence. Carlton slowed down, and for a second Jonah thought he would turn around, but he didn't. He just kept on walking.

"I wasn't laughing!" Jonah said desperately. But Carlton was moving on. Two fallen angels hovered over the boy, whispering quietly into his ears. Carlton was utterly alone. At least, Jonah imagined that's how he felt. The fallen angels had done a masterful job of driving him into that place, using their own words and the actions of the other kids, who probably never stopped to consider what it would be like if they were in the same boat.

And Jonah hadn't done a thing about it.

Images of his mom suddenly flooded his memory. His shoulders began to slump too as he realized how unhappy she would have been with him right about now.

Jonah heard cackling from behind him and spun around. To his left, and up above, on the metal rafters, two fallen angels sat. They looked directly at him and laughed.

"The great Jonah Stone is no more!" one of them called out in a sarcastic voice.

Jonah felt something like steam rise up inside his body. He walked over toward them. "What was that? I couldn't quite hear you way up there in the rafters."

The two creatures looked at each other and hopped off the ledge, spreading their oily black wings and soaring down until they were right in front of him. They were both short and pudgy, a lot like the fallen angel Valack that Jonah had been confronted by in the hallway.

Jonah glanced around the gym. It was completely empty except for them. Mrs. Schaumburg had disappeared into her office.

"I said"—the fatter one leaned in, close to his face—"the great Jonah Stone . . ."

But Jonah wasn't listening. As quickly as he could, he lowered his head, prayed, and entered the hidden realm. He reached for his hip, hoping what he reached for was still there.

When he pulled his hand back, his angelblade glittered. The fallen angels barely had time to scream. He ripped the blade horizontally across the air, slicing through both of them with one blow. Their screams echoed in the cavernous gym for a second, but just like that, they disintegrated into black dust, floating down to the hardwood floor.

Jonah breathed in. It felt good, almost a relief, as he held his blade up in front of him, studying the white glow for a few seconds. Finally, he moved over to the shadows beside the bleachers, sheathed his sword, and reentered the physical world.

It felt good, yes, but his emotions quickly came crashing back down as he remembered that he hadn't helped a friend when he needed it most.

One thing was becoming clear—the more he ignored what Abaddon's evil gang was doing, the less he liked himself.

EIGHT

A STRANGE SIGHT

After he got dressed in his regular clothes again, Jonah searched the hallways for Carlton but couldn't find him. He wanted to catch up with him and really apologize, see how he was doing, and do something.

"Where are you, Carlton?" Jonah muttered under his breath as he walked along the science wing before his next class was to begin. "Aren't you supposed to be around here somewhere?"

But the only thing he found was a handful of students, glancing at him curiously, having heard him talking to himself.

"You all right, big guy?" Tariq said, walking up behind him. "Seems like you're having kind of an 'off' day . . . Talking to yourself again, are you?"

He pulled up alongside Jonah, raising an eyebrow as he held on to both straps of the backpack he was wearing.

Jonah continued scanning the hallway. "I was just looking for Carlton. Have you seen him?"

"Carlton?" Tariq asked, looking puzzled and thinking for a minute. He snapped his fingers. "You mean Professor Carl?"

Jonah rolled his eyes. He'd heard Carlton's nickname before. If he was honest, he had to admit he'd used it once or twice himself. But it wasn't funny anymore. "Yeah, but why don't you just say Carlton Humphries? You wouldn't believe it if I told you what this guy goes through."

"What are you talking about, dude?" Tariq asked. He waved his hand in front of Jonah's eyes, which were still searching the hall. "You okay? It's not mean to call him Professor Carl. I think he likes it."

Jonah snapped his head toward Tariq. "Likes it? You wouldn't believe what the kids just did to him in gym class. He was totally humiliated. And I . . ."

His voice trailed off, and he lost himself in his thoughts again.

Tariq just smiled, blinking at him, and extended his hand forward. "And you . . . ," he said, waiting for him to finish his sentence.

Jonah didn't want to admit out loud that he'd left Carlton to fend for himself. What kind of person was he? Who would do that to someone? These questions were beginning to haunt him.

"Forget it," he finally said—it was too much to try to explain to Tariq. "Let's just get to class."

They walked together past a couple of classroom doors, rounded a corner, and found their room. Valack, the pudgy fallen one, stood beside the entrance to the class. He had his arms folded, scowling as he saw the quarterling come toward him. Jonah hesitated.

"Hey, Tariq," he said, slapping his friend on the shoulder. "I, uh, need to go to the bathroom. I'll be back in here in a few. If the bell rings, just tell Mr. Cooper I'll be back in a sec."

"All right," Tariq answered. "Go get your head straight while you're in there, okay?"

Jonah nodded, barely hearing his friend.

"You destroyed two fallen angels in the gym," Valack said, clearly having trouble containing himself as he stood against the wall. "You're going to cause us to have a little problem here, Stone."

Jonah walked down the hallway and turned into the boys' bathroom. The fallen angel followed him in, and Jonah stood in front of the mirror. Another boy was there, washing his hands. Jonah nodded to him and pretended to wash his hands while waiting for the kid to leave.

"You need to back off," Jonah countered to Valack once the boy walked out and they were alone. "You think I care that I wasted two of your creatures? Good riddance." He eased his hand down to his hip. *Maybe I should do the same thing to you, right now.*

Valack eyed Jonah's hand but didn't seem fazed. "You don't think you can handle us all by yourself, do you?"

Jonah thought he could find some angels to fight with him, but he knew that at the moment, he was by himself. "I don't think I need much help to take you on."

Valack backed up, floating above him and keeping himself just out of range, in case Jonah drew his sword. He clasped his hands together. "Well, that may be true, quarterling. But you have no idea how many of us are here. We own this high school. Haven't you figured that out? There's nothing that happens here that isn't under our control. These kids are ours; they belong to Abaddon. And if you think you can do something about that . . ."

Valack hovered, emboldened by his own words, drawing closer to Jonah again. "Then go ahead and try."

Jonah thought about how many fallen angels he had disintegrated in the name of Elohim. But right now he didn't feel so strong. He eased his hand away from his hip.

"That's better, Jonah," he said in an extra syrupy voice. "You get back to how it was. You play your basketball games and hang out with your friends and have your popularity. We'll take care of our business. We won't bother you. You don't bother us. Hey, if you really think about it, we're helping you out." Valack stood on the ground now, Jonah towering over the pudgy weasel. He grinned, his sharp, yellow-stained fangs dripping. "You get to be cool, and you don't have to worry about Elohim or anything else. So in this next class, why don't you just put your head down and leave everything else in our hands. Okay?"

Valack clapped his hands together, nodded to Jonah, and left the bathroom, leaving Jonah alone.

He felt pulled in two different directions. Why didn't he do something to an underling of Abaddon himself, standing right in front of him, almost daring him to fight?

But then again, why should he get involved, when the only thing that seemed to happen when he did was his mother getting killed?

He pushed open the swinging door of the bathroom and walked toward his classroom, lost inside his swirling head.

Look.

Valack, still in the hallway? He spun to see who had spoken the quiet word. There was no sign of a fallen angel. There was no sign of anyone.

He continued toward his chemistry class, trying to think of an excuse for his tardiness.

Look, Jonah.

He heard the voice again. Jonah spun to look behind him and upward. He turned a complete circle but saw no one. He quickly realized, though, that the voice felt like it was coming from inside him.

Elohim?

He felt a surge of excitement rush through him like electricity, then, in the moment immediately following, a wave of guilt. How long had it been since he had spoken with Him? How long had it been since he had tried to listen to Elohim's voice? How long since he had even prayed at all?

But he was sure. It was His voice.

Look at what? What did Elohim want him to see?

Jonah slid into his seat, trying not to make eye contact with Mr. Cooper, who had paused as he came in, apparently in the middle of a lecture. On the whiteboard at the front of the room, the words "THE BIG BANG" were written in large, black letters.

"Mr. Stone?" he said as Jonah found his seat at the back of the classroom. "Care to elaborate on why you were late?"

Jonah sat down quietly in his chair and set his backpack on the ground, clearing his throat. "I was . . . uh . . . in the bathroom, sir."

Mr. Cooper held up his hands and shook his head. "Never mind. Too much information. Just don't let it happen again, eh? Now, getting back to our topic . . ."

He clasped his hands together, wringing them excitedly. Mr. Cooper wore a short-sleeve shirt with a tie that hit about six inches above his belt. His small glasses made his bald head seem too large for his body. But his face was lit with enthusiasm as he spoke.

"As I was saying, today we are going to begin to discuss the origins of the universe. How we came to be, how our earth was created, and eventually leading us into learning how you and I evolved into who we are today. But first, I want to ask a question. Who thinks they can tell me how our universe began?"

Mr. Cooper paused, his hands behind his back, as he paced back and forth in front of the class. An awkward silence filled the room, and the students began to look at each other. "No one has any ideas at all?"

Something in Jonah wanted to jump up and scream, *"Elohim, of course! Elohim created all of this, and I know Him!"* He felt the words bubbling around inside, but he kept them down. He didn't want to embarrass himself in front of his classmates.

A girl raised her hand across from him.

"Yes, Mandy?"

Jonah leaned forward and looked at the blond, pale girl. He couldn't remember ever having heard her speak before.

She shifted uncomfortably in her seat but looked straight ahead at the teacher. "I believe that the universe began when God created it."

Another student shot a hand up from the back. A boy—Jonah thought his name was Mark—spoke before he could even be called on. "That's what I was going to say too. My dad says that God created everything by speaking words, and then *boom*— things just popped into place."

A long pause filled the room. Mr. Cooper removed his glasses and rubbed the palm of his hand against his eyes. He sighed loudly and began cleaning his glasses on his tie.

Look, Jonah.

Jonah's eyes opened wider. He turned around out of instinct, looking back at the girl sitting directly behind him who was chewing gum, and when she saw him staring at her, she glared back. *What?* she mouthed the word, and Jonah spun back.

He raised his hand now but didn't wait for Mr. Cooper either. "Mr. Cooper, can I be excused?"

The teacher raised an eyebrow at Jonah. "Again, son?"

Jonah held his stomach, grimacing. "Please?"

Mr. Cooper waved his hand at him. "Yes, yes, go ahead. We don't need you having any . . . er . . . troubles in the classroom."

Jonah got up and left, but didn't go to the bathroom. Instead, he stopped just beyond the door, so that no one could see him from inside the room. He looked up and down the hallway, and was satisfied that no one was coming.

He'd finally realized what the voice was asking him to do.

Bowing his head, he prayed for Elohim to allow him into the hidden realm once again. When he opened his eyes, he glanced out the window to make sure it had worked. The grass outside was shimmering with electricity, a sure sign that he was now in the spiritual world, invisible to everyone else.

Jonah walked back into the classroom. He found himself a little nervous, even though he knew no one could see him. He stood in front of his friend Tariq, who sat near the door, and waved his fingers in front of his face. No response. Tariq continued staring straight ahead, unaware of anything happening in the hidden realm.

Mr. Cooper had continued his lecture and clearly was now focusing on the comments from the two students in the back.

"And what we are going to find in our studies on the origins of the universe is that anyone who believes that some kind of higher power had anything to do with it is, well . . ." He paused, chuckling. "Let's just say that they might have something loose up here," he said, pointing to his head and turning his finger in a circle. Most of the other students laughed at this or at least smiled. Jonah noticed that Mandy now stared down at her desk, her cheeks flushed and red. "All of the evidence we have suggests otherwise. That we evolved from simple-celled organisms that were created billions of years ago . . ."

Mr. Cooper continued his lecture, and Jonah stood, listening and watching. But Jonah's eyes were drawn to the students. In the back, the two who had spoken up—Mandy and the other boy—had angels hovering over them, with swords raised. The one above Mandy was a dark-haired female warrior, with silver armor shining. Her face looked very determined and focused. In a similar way, a male angel hovered over the boy. Jonah looked more closely and saw that both of these kids' hearts glowed brightly with the light of Elohim.

The angels' faces drew him in, and their intensity mesmerized him. He'd seen the look on other angels before, when they were attacked in the streets of New York last year. Jonah had seen nothing else in the room to cause alarm, though.

The class full of kids continued listening to Mr. Cooper as he spouted off several more reasons why it was silly and stupid to believe that anything intelligent created earth and the universe.

Just then, a faint noise caught his ear, coming from the doorway. Some kind of screeching, and it grew louder. The students, however, didn't seem to notice. As Jonah looked back at the angels, though, they were bracing themselves. They'd obviously heard it too, the female one nodding at Jonah.

"Get ready," was all she said.

The noise grew louder still, though he still couldn't figure out where it was coming from.

It sounds like . . . birds, he thought. *But why would I be hearing birds right now in the hidden realm?*

Whoosh. Whoosh. Whoosh.

Three creatures swooped in through the door, and Jonah immediately pushed himself backward against Mr. Cooper's bulletin board. They barely fit in the doorway, but they barged in, talons raised.

Jonah felt cold sweat begin to pop out on his forehead and through his shirt. He could hardly bring himself to look.

Their heads were like birds, with long, sharp beaks that reminded him of a hawk or an eagle. Each one had talons that looked razor sharp, extended so that they must have been at least a foot wide. Their upper bodies were covered in black feathers.

The bottom half of their bodies were different, though. The creatures had feet like paws with razor-sharp claws. The rest of their lower halves were like lions, complete with long tails.

Their screeching filled the room as Mr. Cooper continued his lecture.

Whoosh. Whoosh.

More of the creatures entered, each of them landing on a desk in front of a student. Eventually, as Jonah stood in horror and watched, there was one of the winged beasts for each kid—except for the two in the back. The angels were standing in front of Mandy and the boy now, swords blazing, ready to strike. None of the creatures dared to come near them.

"What are they?" Jonah called out to the angels.

The female angel shouted above the screeching. "Ancient creatures, from the pit of Abaddon himself. They are griffins—half eagle, half lion. Notice their eyes?"

Jonah looked at the closest one, who turned toward him and screeched loudly. Its eyes were blazing yellow.

"What are they doing here?"

The angel simply nodded at the creatures.

Look, Jonah.

The kids were still listening, some of them almost spellbound as Mr. Cooper continued to spout off about the foolishness of believing in any kind of God.

If he could only see what I see right now . . .

The griffin closest to him was eyeing the boy it stood before, narrowing its gaze. The kid, a friend of Jonah's from elementary school named Bennett, sat still, writing occasionally in his notebook as the lecture wore on. More correctly, Jonah saw that the creature was eyeing the boy's chest hungrily, like there was something inside he wanted for his own.

The griffin drew closer to the boy and, with one of his talons, reached toward the boy's chest and plunged his claws inside.

All the other creatures did the same with the other students, reaching inside their chests as if they were trying to locate something.

Jonah knew what was there. In the hidden realm, he could see the light of Elohim in each person, proof that they had been made in the image of their Creator. This light, although dim, burned white, as a reminder of the mark of Elohim on each person.

And then, as Jonah watched, paralyzed by the scene in front of him, the griffin latched onto Bennett's inner light.

And pulled it right out of his chest.

The creature held a ball of light in front of him, reflecting in its eyes. It was a glowing sphere, but it beat just like a heart. A few thin tendrils of light reached from the ball back into Bennett's chest as the griffin held it there in its claws.

He glanced up to see the other creatures doing the same with the rest of the students. Reaching into their chests, latching onto the glowing orb of Elohim's light, and then pulling it out.

Each griffin held a teenager's light within its sharply taloned grasp and began to pull at it, squeezing and tugging. Some even lowered their beaks and began to dig into the luminescent orbs. Prying, pecking away, and gnawing at the treasure they held in their hands.

Their goal struck Jonah in a moment of sheer terror—and he now knew why he had heard Elohim's voice, beckoning him to look. Abaddon was after the very hearts of his friends. He knew this already. But seeing it happen, right before his eyes, was something else altogether.

Maybe this was happening in every other classroom in the school. *Does this go on every day? Is this what we're facing? Is this what goes on in this place? Why haven't I noticed this before?*

The griffin holding on to Tariq's light chewed away, trying to loosen it from the tendrils that held it within his chest. The creature glanced up at Jonah with its beady yellow eyes and seemed to almost smile. *There's nothing you can do about this,* it seemed to be saying.

Jonah turned to the angels. "I don't know what your orders are, sitting there like that while this is happening. But I can't let this go on. Not right here in front of me."

He pulled his angelblade from his hip, but the griffins were so busy feeding on his classmates they didn't even look up.

Jonah held the blade high, then crashed it down on the closest griffin to him. A horrible screeching filled the air as the sword sliced into its wing. It fell to the ground in a lump of feathers and fur.

The one holding on to Tariq loosened its grip, turned, and charged at him with its hooked beak open. But Jonah was ready. He sliced into the beast, sending it to the floor.

He shouted at the others, bracing himself for another attack.

The rest of the creatures let go of his classmates and headed toward him. But instead of attacking him, they soared out of the room. The last two screeched again at him, grabbed the two fallen beasts in their claws, and followed the others.

Jonah breathed heavily as he watched the light of Elohim return to his classmates' chests.

He wasn't sure how long he stood there, letting his breathing slow down and watching the classroom. It was as if everything were happening in slow motion.

"Maybe someone should check on Jonah and see if he's all right."

Mr. Cooper's words broke through his haze. Tariq hopped up from his desk, always eager for a reason to miss class, even for a minute or two.

"No problem, Mr. C. I'll go see if he fell in."

A few of the kids laughed, and Jonah had to rush out of the room fast to avoid colliding with his friend.

He moved quickly around the corner, to get ahead of Tariq and return to the physical world. Everything returned in him except his mind, which was squarely stuck back on what he'd seen, the voice that had told him to look, and what he was supposed to do now.

✧

11:09 p.m.

Hey E,

I got your last e-mail—don't worry. Thanks. I'll try to remember to hug Dad for you. Things around here are . . . getting weird. Especially at school. I'm trying to be normal and just fit in, but lately it seems around every corner there's some fallen angel doing something bad. Not sure why they just won't leave me alone. A crazy thing happened earlier today that I'm sure would make you flip out . . .

I miss Mom a lot. And I guess I miss you guys too . . . sort of. Punch Jeremiah in the arm for me.

Oh, and tell Julia I said hi, okay?

Jonah

PART II

CONSEQUENCES

In my distress I called to the LORD, and he

answered me. From deep in the realm of the dead

I called for help, and you listened to my cry.

Jonah 2:2 NIV

PART II

CONSEQUENCES

NINE

VISIT IN DARKNESS

The long, black limousine eased through the streets, quietly navigating around the cabs, bicycles, and, of course, the masses of pedestrians. The man in the back of the car gazed at the city flashing past him, his hand rubbing his chin. The multicolored lights reflected through the darkened windows, changing his face from yellow, to blue or red, then yellow again.

The driver adjusted his rearview mirror so that his eyes were now visible.

"Almost there."

The man nodded, tugging on his cuff links until they showed from underneath his jacket.

"What would you like me to do, sir?" asked the man with silver curly hair sitting beside him, whose muscular arms seemed about to rip through his jacket. He felt for the weapon hidden underneath his clothes.

The man continued watching the city, running his hand along his slick hair, pressing it down along his head.

"Let me handle it," he said.

The silver-haired man nodded respectfully. "Yes, sir."

The car eased into a parking spot along the waterway in front of a mega yacht, a monstrosity of extravagance, sleek gray, its edges barely distinguishable from the dark waters it floated in. A series of pale blue lights shone in the back, illuminating the water in a ghostly way.

The man checked his watch. 3:46 a.m. He looked upward, along the sides of the great boat, to the top platform. A figure stood there, arms outstretched on the rails, looking down at the street. Four security guards were stationed at equal distances apart, each holding a weapon, eyes also trained below.

The man in the car smiled as he watched them. What they didn't know was that up above, creatures were circling.

The driver opened the back door, and the man walked down the dock until he came to the ramp leading him over to the yacht.

Two men in black suits stepped through the yacht door, standing on the gangplank in front of him. They both held handguns by their sides. He looked up, meeting them in the eye.

"Gentlemen, good evening," he said.

They looked surprised and glanced at each other.

"Sir," one of them said, holstering his weapon. "Uh . . . it's late. We weren't expecting you."

"I thought it would be a nice night for a visit," the man said, breathing the cold air in deeply and smiling with all of his teeth. They looked curiously at each other again.

"Yes, sir," the guard said.

The man walked closer, reaching forward to the guard, and straightened the man's tie. He slapped him on the shoulder. "You're going to let me on board, aren't you, Jerry?"

The guard's knees buckled, and for a moment, it looked like he was going to lose his dinner over the railing. Before he regained his composure, the man in the suit had somehow slipped past them, walking through the doorway. The other one appeared suddenly dazed, as if he didn't quite know where he was.

"Don't worry, men, I sometimes have that effect on people," he said. "I won't be long. Not very long at all."

He entered the ship and went up three flights of steps, which led to the top deck. The figure still stood against the railing, looking down, unaware of the footsteps until they were directly behind him.

"Vitaly!" the man called out, his arms open wide as if he expected a hug. Vitaly jerked upward and spun around. A blue bathrobe was draped across his large frame, and slippers were on his feet.

"Mr. Prince," he said, his thick accent shaking. "I wasn't expecting visitors this late. What brings the special advisor to the United Nations out on a night such as this?"

Mr. Prince walked toward the man, still smiling from ear to ear.

"I just thought it was a nice evening for a little stroll on a boat," he answered, his eyes twinkling. "Looks like you thought the same thing. I guess great minds do think alike, Vitaly."

Vitaly nodded, his eyes cutting upward to the guards stationed above and watching closely. "Yes, well, it is awfully late, and I'm getting tired." He laughed softly. "I sometimes come out here when I can't sleep, to clear my head. But I was just getting ready to turn in for the evening."

"Yes, yes," Mr. Prince said, studying Vitaly and not moving. "I guess it is late, isn't it? I hadn't really noticed."

Vitaly nodded, walking past him toward the door. "You won't be offended, sir, if I don't ask you inside tonight? My guards can show you the way out." Whether it was a threat or just an offer, the top deck guards had taken a few steps toward them, obviously having been alerted by the men below.

"Vitaly," he chided, "I've come all this way to visit with you. The least you could do would be to show me some of that famous Russian hospitality, huh?"

Vitaly froze in mid-stride, his shoulders slumping as he turned back around.

"What is it that you have come here for, Mr. Prince?"

He folded his arms and stood on the deck of his yacht, waiting.

Mr. Prince chuckled. "I guess that's all the hospitality I'm going to get tonight. No matter. I guess I have come here not so much for pleasure, after all, but for business."

Vitaly raised his eyebrow and stood a little taller. "Why not back in my office, in the morning? Why out here like this?"

Mr. Prince shrugged. "Some conversations are fit for the ambassador's office and some aren't. You, of all people, should know that, eh, Vitaly?"

Vitaly held the man's gaze for a few seconds but then looked down. He wondered what Mr. Prince actually knew. His past was checkered, but the fact was that not many men rose to his position untainted by the ways of the world. Vitaly decided he must be bluffing.

"I don't know what you mean," he said gruffly. "But please, state your business. The night—and my opportunity to sleep—are both disappearing rapidly."

"Very well, Vitaly," Mr. Prince said, and his smile began to fade. "I came here tonight to tell you something, and then there's something I want to show you. You see, you and I are going to be getting to know each other a little better. We're going to become…

very close. I have some plans, big ones, and you're going to help me accomplish them."

He locked eyes with Vitaly as he spoke, and Vitaly found that he couldn't look away. "I'm going to help you with your plans?" he asked, trying to manage a smile of his own. "What exactly are you talking about?"

"I'll be letting you in on things along the way," Mr. Prince answered. "Now all I need to know is—are you with me or not?"

Vitaly rubbed the top of his head. His thoughts were suddenly feeling thick, dense. Special advisor to the United Nations or not, who was this man to come and tell him what he would or would not do? And yet, as much as he tried to form those words in his mouth, they wouldn't come.

"I'll take that silence as a yes," Mr. Prince exclaimed, grabbing him by the shoulders and pulling him uncomfortably close. "Now, I said I had something to show you, didn't I?"

Vitaly could only nod, mesmerized by the strange look in Mr. Prince's eyes. Those eyes began to change as he looked deeper in. Vitaly's mouth dropped open.

The eyes weren't eyes anymore. They grew larger and larger— or was he simply drawing closer? It was impossible to tell.

"Ooh," Vitaly said, beginning to smile curiously as he looked on. He could see nothing else now except an image in front of him, deep within the eyes of Mr. Prince.

His face grew brighter as he stared, his smile grew larger, and a speckle of drool left his lip and dribbled down his chin, going unnoticed. Suddenly, he was a kid on Christmas morning.

"Are you enjoying what you see, Vitaly?" Mr. Prince cooed, knowing the answer already. Vitaly could barely nod, he was so taken by the vision. "Good."

Mr. Prince blinked, and Vitaly lurched back, shaking his head.

"Don't...," he whispered, holding his hand up to Mr. Prince's face. "Where ... where did it go?"

His face drooped now, the mysterious image suddenly disappearing. He was back on his yacht, looking at the black eyes of Mr. Prince.

"I can't show you too much of that at once," Mr. Prince answered with a grin. "Might make you turn to jelly inside. But I can assure you that if you stay with me and do what I say, everything you saw will be yours."

Vitaly gulped. He nodded slowly. "Everything?"

Mr. Prince leaned forward. "And more, my friend. And more. Now, time for me to go."

He extended his hand, and Vitaly took it.

"Ahhh!" he said, yanking his hand back suddenly. "A shock!"

He rubbed the palm of his hand and stared up at him.

"Must have been static electricity," Mr. Prince said, shrugging. He shoved his hands in his pockets. "Vitaly, I'll be in touch."

With that, he turned and walked through the door, watched by the man who looked uncertainly at him, still rubbing his hand, while his mind was being poisoned by the images he had seen.

TEN

IN PURSUIT

Tap, tap, tap.

Eliza opened her eyes halfway, and for a moment tried to remember where she was. Where had she been? Walking through the woods with her mother, talking about something, when she heard a woodpecker tapping against a tree . . .

She blinked at her surroundings. She was in her own bed in her small room at the convent. She'd been dreaming. Turning her head, she saw Julia was still sleeping soundly in the bed across the room.

Tap, tap, tap. A little louder. The bird?

No, Eliza. Get the door. Her alarm clock read 4:13 a.m. She rubbed her eyes as her bare feet hit the floor.

"Eliza!" came a hushed whisper. "Are you awake?"

She rolled her eyes. Of course. Swinging open the door, she saw her brother standing in front of her in his pajamas, slippers on his feet.

"Do you know what time it is?" she asked. "Are you crazy? Why aren't you asleep?"

He shrugged his shoulders, shifting on his feet. "I keep waking up."

She stared at the ceiling, wondering if he'd had the same dream she had. "Well, just roll over and try harder." She started to shut the door in his face.

"I just keep thinking about her," he said, peering at her with his round eyes.

Eliza sighed, resting her back against the door frame. "Mom, you mean?"

He nodded. "I saw her, Eliza. I really did, and I just keep thinking that she's out there somewhere, alone, and wanting to be with us."

"Jeremiah," she said, rubbing her eyes. "We've been through this already. It was a mistake. You thought you saw someone who looked like her, but it couldn't have been Mom. It's just impossible."

"I don't know," he pushed. "You weren't there. You didn't see what I saw. I saw her face, Eliza. I looked straight at her. And she saw me. I promise, she looked right at me."

"And then?" she asked.

He sighed. "Then she walked down the street, away from me. But she wanted me to follow her, I could tell. And if you'd only have let me keep going . . ."

"I was trying to save your tail and get us out of the mess you got us all into!" she said, steeling her jaw. She was too tired to have patience with Jeremiah anymore.

Jeremiah turned his eyes toward his feet again. He looked so lost.

"I'm sorry," she said quietly. "Jeremiah, I know you miss her terribly. I do too. But our minds, they do weird things when we're under stress and need rest. Maybe you just need to get back in bed, and you'll think about it more clearly in the morning. In fact, why don't you sleep in a little bit longer? I'll cover for you at breakfast if anyone asks where you are."

She began to close the door when he stopped it with his hand. "Maybe you're right. But I still can't get the picture of her out of my head."

"Good night, Jeremiah," she said, managing a smile. "We'll talk about it in the morning."

She shut the door softly and waited behind it until she heard his feet slipping across the old wooden floors toward the stairwell.

Climbing back into bed, she pulled her blanket up around her neck, letting the warmth cover her. She closed her eyes and tried to go back to sleep.

4:29. The glowing red letters of the clock glared at her.

4:34. She watched it, unable to get her eyes to shut. 4:36. 4:37.

Sighing loudly, Eliza threw her blanket off and stood up.

"Jeremiah, you're going to pay for this," she muttered to herself. She loved her sleep, but she knew that once she was awake, she was awake. She might as well make good use of her time.

Eliza got dressed without waking Julia up, pulling on her jeans, zipping up a black hoodie, and grabbing her backpack. She'd decided to head downstairs to the quarterling lounge for a little early morning reading.

But as she walked down the hallway, toward the steps, a feeling moved so strongly within her that she stopped, mid-stride.

Check on him.

It wasn't that she heard an audible voice, but somehow, the feeling inside her spoke into her heart.

"Elohim?" she whispered, waiting and listening.

Check on him.

She was sure Jeremiah was back in his room, sound asleep. But she moved up the stairs, not down. At least she could stop by his room and check.

Not wanting to wake him, she turned the door handle to his room as quietly as she could. She would see him lying there, sprawled out on his bed, and then she'd head downstairs and enjoy the silence of the study room.

His roommate, Carlo, was asleep, legs hanging off the bed, head stuffed underneath the pillow. He was snoring.

She stuck her head in just enough to see Jeremiah's bed. Covers were strewn everywhere, and his pillow had fallen on the floor. Eliza had to blink several times before she realized that he wasn't there.

"Jeremiah!" she said in a hoarse whisper.

Settle down, Eliza. Maybe he's in the bathroom or couldn't sleep either and went downstairs for a cup of grape juice.

But the feeling inside her stomach spoke something else.

Eliza tapped lightly on the bathroom door.

"Jeremiah!" she hissed, finally cracking, then pushing the door wide open, finding no one there. Her heart began to beat a little faster.

She bounded down the steps to the first level of the convent and rounded the corner of the hallway as quickly as she could, coming to the door that led one more flight down. The basement room that had been set aside for the quarterlings to have a place to come, hang out, and study was at the bottom of a long set of steps.

Surely he's down here shooting baskets or something. The basketball hoop against the far wall was popular with Jeremiah, who could be found practicing his free throws at any moment of the day.

But no balls were bouncing, and when she found the room empty, her heart began thumping even faster.

"This is so irrational, Jeremiah . . ." She scowled, stomping back up the steps.

He'd gone looking for their mom.

She glanced at the clock on her phone. It was 5:01, and she didn't want to wake up any of the others. If anything came along, she could handle it. Besides, he was probably out just wandering the streets, trying to find where they were the other day.

Eliza left through the front door of the convent and stood on the street for a second, pulling her hood over her head as she shivered in the cold, dark air. She looked up but could see no light yet, no sign of the sunrise to come, no shadow of the angels she was sure guarded the street and probably saw her now. She waved up to the darkness, if for no other reason than to say, "Hey, I'm not sneaking out, you know . . . My brother may have, but not me!"

She stuck her hands in her jacket pockets and began to walk, keeping her eyes moving, looking for any sign of a boy. And signs of anything else too. She wondered if it would be a good idea to enter the hidden realm. Then she could see if the enemy was around. But she also thought she might need to ask people along the street if they'd seen a young boy by himself. For now, she would stay in the physical world.

Her feet moved as briskly as she could make them. Jonah and Jeremiah weren't the only ones who'd grown taller. She had sprouted up a full three inches in the last six months alone, and her long legs could cover some ground. Eliza turned her steps south, city block after city block passing underneath her feet with no sign of Jeremiah.

Could he have made it all the way to the warehouse where they were the other day? She mulled that over in her mind as she walked, fiddling with her cell phone in her pocket. She wasn't even sure he knew where it was. After all, they'd wandered into it while fighting the fallen angels, and their own angels had flown them back to the safety of the convent.

Maybe she was going on a wild goose chase. *He probably is back in bed at the convent. I just missed him somehow.*

But she couldn't just turn around and go back now. Once again, though, she found herself on a mission to recover her lost brother, and she began to feel the heat of frustration rise up around her neck with every empty city block. He was foolish to go out alone, but it was typical Jeremiah. With each step, she pictured the worst. Jeremiah, backed against the wall, fallen angels surrounding him, unable to defend himself against an evil gang of them.

She knew too, though, the pain he was feeling. As irrational as it was, she knew the draw of somehow finding their mom was powerful.

With that thought, she decided to enter the hidden realm. She prayed silently as she walked along and disappeared from sight.

"Jeremiah!" she called out down the vacant street. "Jeremiah!"

No response, no sight of him. But that didn't mean she went unheard.

Three fallen angels rounded the corner right in front of her.

She froze. But they were too close for her to try to jump inside a doorway or down an alley. They had heard her.

"Looking for someone, are we, Eliza Stone?" one of them said.

"Oh, are you surprised we know your name?" another one

jumped in, seeing the look of shock on her face. "You quarterlings are well known to all of us. Don't you know the kind of reward I'd get if I brought you in?"

The fallen angel in the middle elbowed him, glaring. "What do you mean, you? If anyone's going to bring her in, it's going to be me."

Eliza gathered herself. "If I could interrupt for a second, there's a slight problem with your thought process here."

The one on her left piped up. "Really? What's that now, girl?"

She reached down beside her and pulled hard across her hip. "This!"

A blazing sword appeared out of nowhere, shimmering a jewel-like green as she pointed it toward their faces.

"Mind letting me pass?" she said in the boldest way she knew.

Instead, the three fallen ones pulled out their swords, blazing fire red, each one swirling with hot flames. "We have one of those too, you know," the middle one said, grinning and tossing his sword back and forth from his left hand to his right.

Eliza took a step back, feeling the weight of her angelblade in her hand. She hadn't had hers nearly as long as Jonah had, and boy, did she wish he were here now. But still, she had been able to practice with it and hoped now that her extra training with Marcus and Taryn had been enough.

It was also a good thing that she'd been able to learn how to produce the shield of faith with one hand.

She raised her left hand in the air, and immediately the white shell of light sprung from her fingers, an orb that encircled her, all the way down to her feet.

"Nice trick, little girl," one of the Fallen said, moving toward her. "But why don't we see how your little shield holds up to three demon blades?"

He moved toward her, raising his sword with the intention of bringing it crashing down on her shield. But as he did, she moved quickly, swinging the tip of her blade through the air.

It sliced through the fallen angel's arm.

"Aarrghhhh!" he cried, grabbing his arm and writhing in pain as he fell to the ground. While the others only watched, she drove her blade into his chest.

"Well, how about that?" she said, almost to herself and almost as surprised at her success as the other two fallen angels were. She held the blade up to them. "Which one of you is next?"

The ashes of the first fallen angel were disappearing underneath their feet as they both swung, their blades crashing into her shield at the same time. She felt the weight of their blows, wincing, hunching down, and absorbing them. They didn't wait to see if she would recover. They began to strike her shield again and again and again.

Eliza began to back up, forced to retreat. Finally, she caught her footing, bracing herself, and pushed forward with the shield and everything she had. She had to find some room to use the only real weapon she had, her sword.

She forced them back just enough. Raising her sword, she swung again. This time, it was met by the fiery blade of the fallen angel, and a shower of green and red sparks rained in the air. Her arm was still up and her shield still raised, but it was growing weaker.

Remembering a move she'd seen Marcus do the other day in class, in one motion she pulled her sword back, spun, and brought the angelblade slicing through the air from the other direction.

It did the trick. Catching the fallen one off guard, she hit him on the other side, sending the sword straight through his midsection. His scream was muffled as soon as his mouth and the rest of him turned into vaporized dust.

She turned her attention to the one fallen angel left, waving her sword toward him. He held his in front of him, and they began to circle one another. Dropping her left hand, her shield disappeared.

"Where's my brother?" she asked, glaring at the ugly creature. "Did you see a kid pass through here not long ago? Tell me, and maybe I won't kill you."

The fallen one spat on the ground. "He's dead!"

She swung her sword as hard as she could with both hands. "Liar!"

He blocked her advance and countered with his own strike. They began to wale away at one another, back and forth, crashing their blades together, each trying to find an advantage. He was making huge swings, and Eliza knew that if she could avoid them long enough, that may be her chance.

He swung again, and she cried out, pretending to hurt her arm. The fallen one saw an opportunity. Raring his blade back, he swung for her head.

Eliza ducked, and just as she did, she delivered her blade upward, into the arm holding his sword. The arm—and the sword itself—dropped onto the pavement, the hand around the hilt disintegrating, leaving the blade glittering alone.

The fallen angel stepped backward, holding his arm and howling in pain. Eliza was quick to move on him. She took advantage of his lack of balance, and kicking his foot out from underneath him, she pushed his chest, and he fell onto the ground. Immediately, she put her knee on his abdomen and her sword at his throat.

"You are the most awful-smelling creature I've ever been

around," she said, wrinkling her nose. He was writhing in pain, and she looked at the wound. The blade had cut him just below the shoulder, and she figured she didn't have much time left.

"You were lying about my brother, weren't you?" she said, leaning in. "He's not dead, is he? Tell me the truth!"

He sputtered, a gargling sound in the back of his throat, eyes shining a bright yellow as he tried to laugh. Only it came out as a wheezy cough.

"Don't you know," he asked weakly, "that lying is what we do?"

She grabbed him by his armor and shook him. "Did you see him? Where did he go? Tell me!"

He coughed again, laughing, and then, as she held him, she felt her grip loosen. Her knee hit the pavement beneath her, and she watched as he slowly disappeared. His remains fell underneath her and then seeped into the street.

Eliza sat on her knees on the cold pavement, gathering herself until she could stand and continue looking for Jeremiah.

ELEVEN

BACK AT THE WAREHOUSE

Eliza approached the warehouse with no small degree of caution. She saw the underground driveway they had emerged from in the yellow moving truck and felt her stomach lurch as she remembered what it felt like to sit in the back with her brother, wondering if the awful creatures were flying outside.

She had remained in the hidden realm as she walked, but thankfully hadn't come across any more fallen angels. She had chalked up the encounter with those three as bad luck, and she was grateful she'd been able to destroy them before they could alert any of the rest of their horde. The last thing she or Jeremiah needed was a group of fallen angels chasing them when they were out alone at night with no backup.

She felt her anger rise toward Jeremiah again. When was he going to learn that his actions caused other people problems too?

Eliza looked up and down the street, and finally convinced no one was watching her, made her way across. She looked for any sign of him but found none. Eyeing the opening that led into the parking deck below, she figured she would give it a try.

Although it was just beginning to grow light outside, the garage was lit by the same fluorescent lights. She walked in, hoping to find her little brother wandering around.

Instead, she found an empty lot, except for a handful of cars parked in random spots.

She sighed, adjusting her glasses. "Come on, Jeremiah. Where are you?" *Maybe we should give him a cell phone. It would make this a whole lot easier.*

"Jeremiah?" she called out as loudly as she thought she could. *"Jeremiah?"*

Eliza walked through the empty lot, trying to put herself into the shoes of her nine-year-old brother. She saw the steps to the right, leading up to the warehouse above, and knew that was the only place she had left to search.

When she arrived at the top of the stairs, she stopped to survey the scene. The conveyor belts weren't moving on the factory floor yet, and there were a handful of workers milling about. It appeared as if the workday was about to begin in the warehouse.

Her eyes were drawn to the door at the end of the conveyor belts to her left. There was some kind of disturbance going on. Two men were hunched over, struggling with something. Or was it someone?

Eliza was still in the hidden realm, so she stopped breathing when she saw the fallen angels swoop in from all corners of the place. They hovered over the men, encircling them in a frenzy, several of them leaning in, mouths to their ears.

She heard the scream and knew it in an instant.

"Jeremiah!"

The only thing she saw was the back of his head as he strained against the two large men in suits, who were dragging him out of the warehouse and through the small room, toward the door that led into the alleyway.

Eliza began to run, praying as she went to reenter the visible world. But by the time she got to the door, they had yanked him through it, even though he was resisting and flailing himself around.

She burst through the doorway so fast that she tripped, falling across the cold pavement. Her cheek scraped against the hard ground, but she didn't notice the scratches or the blood.

"Jeremiah!" she called out again.

But it was too late.

She watched a black car speed toward the busy street ahead. Before it disappeared into an ocean of other vehicles, she saw a boy turn his head, looking back through the rear window.

"Jeremiah!"

Eliza looked on helplessly as she found herself standing alone in the middle of the quiet city street. She reached into her back pocket and pulled out her phone.

TWELVE

CENTER COURT

Jonah was walking through the school corridor, and he was alone. His backpack hung heavily on his back as he found himself lost in his thoughts yet again. He couldn't stop thinking about what had happened at school the day before. The kids taunting Carlton, their blind following of whatever they were told, regardless of the truth, the outright arrogance of their science teacher, and those monsters attacking them. He didn't want to see another one of those as long as he lived.

"Jonah."

The word spoken to him was like rushing, cool water. He suddenly noticed that no lights were on in the hall. A faint white glow came from only one room, the next one ahead on his right.

He moved forward, feeling the rush of relief still in his heart from hearing his name. But something in him resisted, and he peered into the doorway with his hands stuffed in his pockets, hesitant.

A man sat on the edge of the teacher's desk, his feet dangling off the floor. His hair was brown and neatly cut, and his eyes sparkled. He wore a blue button-down shirt and khaki pants, typical male teacher wardrobe, but Jonah hadn't seen this teacher before.

"Hi, Jonah," he said in that same voice that washed over Jonah like a cool rain on a dry summer day. The teacher beckoned to Jonah, "Come on over and sit with me."

Jonah stepped into the doorway but stopped, fingering the strap of his backpack. It felt so good to hear his name spoken by this man. Jonah stared at his face, which almost seemed to be radiating a warm, gold light. Jonah couldn't take his eyes away, and yet, there was something inside him still that wanted to turn and leave.

"I know you're upset," the familiar man said. "And you have every right to be. You've been wandering around in the wilderness, afraid, and you feel alone. Am I wrong about that?"

He slid off the desk and stood in front of Jonah, hands in his pockets. Jonah flinched, feeling the tug-of-war within him grow. He wanted to go and sit with the man. He reminded Jonah of someone . . . someone from his past. But he couldn't place it.

But another, darker part of him wanted him to stay right where he was.

Jonah didn't move, either forward or backward.

The man took another step toward him.

"Jonah." He said his name again kindly, almost like his father would, as if the very word were sweet to his mouth. "Come in. Let's talk. You're hurting, and I can help."

"You haven't helped me yet," Jonah said, the forcefulness of his own words surprising him.

The man looked pained, almost as if these words physically hurt. He looked Jonah in his eyes, still radiating love and acceptance. "My offer of love to you has always been there, and I've never left you alone. Even though I know you've felt alone. Very much so."

Jonah sighed. It was true, so true, and the words resonated with him deeply. He had felt like no one was there, and no one could help. But whose fault was that? He had tried, for at least a month after his mom died, to find help with his father, with people in the church, his friends . . . and most of all, Elohim Himself. And what had he heard when he cried out for help? Nothing. Nothing but awful, hardened silence.

He steeled himself, feeling his heart turn a shade darker.

"No one has been there for me," he said, glaring. "I tried, after she died. I tried, and you know it. And no one was there for me. Especially not Him!" He pointed upward, toward the ceiling, unable to even say His name.

"One day you will see, Jonah," the man said. "One day you will know. Elohim has a purpose for you, and yes, a purpose, even in this. He wants you back. He is calling you to Himself, and a day will come when you will see. Your mother's death was—"

But Jonah didn't want to hear any more—no more about his mom's death and how it had a purpose and there was a reason behind it. He didn't want anyone, not even this man, to speak of his mother again. The rope inside him, the one both sides were pulling, was tugged hard, and one side gave in.

He put his hands on his ears and backed out of the room.

Jonah walked down the hallway again, in a haze, ignoring the pleas inside to return to the room, to sit with the gentle man, to pour his heart out to him and to let him help. He hardened himself against that and stepped forward.

When he rounded the corner in the darkened hallway, another voice spoke into the emptiness of the corridor and his heart.

"*Jonah Stone . . .*"

This was a voice he recognized too, but waves of peace didn't swell in his heart this time. Instead, his heart began to race, a vague sense of dread overtaking him. He quickly forgot about the man in the other room, all those feelings swept aside.

A paler light came from another doorway ahead.

Jonah stepped toward it, somehow enticed and frightened by the voice at the same time. He pushed away the urge to run, instead wondering what he might find in this room.

"*Come on in. Don't be afraid, my son . . .*"

Jonah stepped into the classroom, only to find that it wasn't a classroom at all. It was clammy and damp, moss growing where the ceiling once was and along the ground. The sides of the room were like a cave, or a dark jungle, vines and branches hanging from the ceiling. It smelled musty, almost like the boys' locker room after a hard-fought game.

Sitting in the middle of the room, in a plush chair, was a man wearing a white suit with a matching hat and a black tie. A neatly trimmed goatee covered his face.

Jonah's stomach dropped.

"Well, grandson, it's nice to see you here," the man said, his eyes gleaming.

Victor Grace. It was Victor Grace, who had been destroyed underneath the streets of New York. Victor was a fallen angel, who was also his mother's father.

"But you . . . you're supposed to be . . ."

"What?" he said. "Dead?" He began to chuckle. "You know that kind of thinking is what I would expect of a human, Jonah, but not from you, not with someone with so much power and ability. Surely you know better."

Jonah stood in the doorway, his mind racing. He wanted to lash out, to reach for his angelblade and destroy this fallen one who had started his family on this whole awful path. He had manipulated and used his grandmother, whom Jonah had never known. They had married, but Victor had left as soon as his new bride was pregnant. She had had the baby all alone. That baby, of course, was his mother, Eleanor.

"You'll never be my grandfather, Marduk," Jonah said, calling Victor by his real name.

He smiled at Jonah for a few seconds, tugging at his lip. "You can't change the past," he said. "You can't change the present, and you know what?" He tapped his fingers on his knee for a moment, glancing up somewhere above Jonah. "You can't even change the future."

He smiled broadly again, as if this were the best news he'd ever heard. Jonah felt his heart sink. Everything within him wanted to change. He wanted to be different, to run, to change everything about his past, to have a different life.

"But let me tell you one thing," Marduk said, standing up now as he held a single finger aloft. "Leaving that room down there, with that other guy in it . . . that powerless, weak, sappy man . . ." He moved forward as he spoke these words, and Jonah felt locked into the ground, powerless to move. "You did the right thing."

The man grabbed Jonah by the shoulders. Jonah flinched at the icy touch of Marduk's fingers through his shirt. He pulled Jonah close to him in a cold embrace. "Yes," Marduk continued, "don't worry about him. You will have everything you ever wanted right here with me."

Jonah felt the man's fingers on his back, like ice picks,

beginning to dig. They burrowed into his shirt, and then beyond. Jonah felt the ice shoot through his body, as if his bloodstream had become a frozen river. He was freezing, and he felt faint. His mind wandered hazily, as he wondered when he would feel the ice-pick fingers pushing all the way through his chest.

"Jonah . . ." He heard the voice again, but it wasn't coming from Marduk. The voice from down the hallway, just barely, in his ears again. It held just enough warmth to allow his mind to think again.

"Aaaaahhh!" Jonah cried, and with all his strength, he pushed against Marduk's chest, feeling his talons rip out from his back. "Let go!"

Jonah went sprawling back on the ground. Victor Grace laughed, standing over him.

"There's nothing you can do, Jonah," he said. "Nothing you can do to change anything! Best bet for you is to keep on running!"

Jonah pushed himself away from the door and back into the hall and did just what Marduk said.

He ran.

Jonah awoke later on the floor of his room, just below the set of bunk beds. His head pounded, and his body felt weak. His legs were sore, as if he'd actually been sprinting. He had been, right? His mind was foggy, and he lay on the carpet, some of the fibers from it sticking to his lower lip.

He suddenly saw the image of Victor Grace again, and pushing himself up, he had to stop himself from running out of his own hallway, down the steps, and out of the house.

"It was a dream, Jonah," he said out loud to himself. "Just another dream. It was nothing. Nothing. It was nothing at all."

He told himself the same thing over and over again as he took his shower, leaning against the tile wall, letting hot water course over his body, especially his back, which, dream or not, still felt as cold as ice.

Jonah continued telling himself the same thing as he ate his cereal, mumbling the words over and over again.

"What was that, son?"

Jonah continued to stare into the bowl of milk in front of him, picking the last bits of marshmallow from it, lost in his thoughts.

"Jonah," Benjamin said. "Did you hear me, son?"

At the word *son*, Jonah snapped out of his daze and glared up at his father. Victor Grace had used that word too. He had to blink a few times to remind himself again where he was.

It was only a dream, Jonah. A dream.

"Yeah, yeah, sorry," he said. "I was just . . . going over something for a test for school today. Memorization technique, you know?"

Benjamin set his mug down across from Jonah and sat down. Propping his elbows on the table, he sat for a minute in silence, occasionally scratching his beard, which had grown shaggy and unkempt. He looked as tired as Jonah felt.

"We need to talk, Jonah." His father took a big gulp of coffee from his mug.

Jonah pushed his bowl away. "I have to get to the bus stop. I don't want to be—"

"Son!" his father raised his voice, then backed off, gathering himself. "Son . . . I don't care about you being late to school right now. It's more important that you and I . . ."

Jonah looked at him, raising an eyebrow as he checked his

watch. "That we what?"

"Talk," his dad said, breathing heavily through his nose. "We haven't talked in so long, and I know that you're upset, and you miss your mother like crazy . . ."

Jonah leaned back, crossing his arms in his chair and looking down at his feet while his dad continued.

"It's just that, well, it's been almost a year since Eleanor died, the hardest year of our lives, without a doubt. But it's been almost a year . . ."

"So?" Jonah asked. He felt his temperature rising, and he was suddenly ready for a fight.

Benjamin took his glasses off, blew on them, and began cleaning them on a napkin. When he spoke, he did so softly. "So, yes, it's been almost a year, not very long when you consider the loss you have had. But you need to make progress. You need to take steps. And all I see right now is you running in place. You're still here, for goodness' sake! I have allowed that. I have given you your space. I've tried to understand what you're going through." He sighed, putting his glasses back on. "But I'm not so sure that hasn't been a mistake."

Jonah felt the boiling hot bubbles of contempt rise from somewhere deep inside. Tears began forcing their way from his eyes, and he pushed back from the table and stood. "You don't even know me. You don't know what I'm going through. You think I haven't taken any steps? You don't think I'm making any progress? Look at yourself!" He pointed to his dad. "You stay locked in your study. You wander around the house. You don't even shave your beard anymore. You're a total mess. And you want to give me advice about what to do?"

Jonah backed away from the table and grabbed his backpack, slinging it on his back. He turned around just before he reached the door. "I'm here because I want to be here. I don't want to go back to New York. That's fine for Eliza and Jeremiah, but that's not me anymore. That's not who I am!"

He heard his father stand, move toward the door, and call out, "Jonah! I want to talk more tonight, okay?"

∽

Jonah tried to think it all through on the bus as he stared out the window on the way to school, but he didn't know what to make of it. He knew his dream had been more than a regular dream. It had been a while since he'd even admitted to himself the truth. That he was a quarterling. That he was a prophet of Elohim. That he was different.

But figuring out what to do with the dream was harder, because every time he thought about the conversation with the man in the first room, he just felt more frustrated and angry.

Jonah slammed his hand against the side of the bus lightly.

His father was right about one thing. He was definitely stuck.

The rest of the day went no better. The creatures were everywhere. If possible, it seemed as though they had doubled overnight. He tried to tell himself he was just more attuned to them, but he wasn't so sure. He didn't even have to be in the hidden realm to see them everywhere. He resisted stepping into the spiritual world, afraid of what he might find if he did. Fallen angels were whispering in some students' ears, tormenting others, and driving kids apart from one another and into loneliness and isolation. Jonah saw it happening in front of him, but he was paralyzed. Every time he thought of his mother, that old anger spewed and boiled inside and he turned away.

Finally, the last bell rang, and Jonah headed to the gym to get ready for that night's basketball game.

Tariq caught up to him. "Ready for a big game tonight, my man?" He held out his hand, and Jonah slapped it.

"At this point, Tariq," he said, "I'm ready for anything other than going home."

"Trouble with your dad or something?" Tariq asked.

Jonah grimaced. "Is it that obvious?"

Tariq shrugged his shoulders. "Let's just call it an educated guess, that's all. But whatever is going on, you really should try to fix it. Your dad is cool, and you two have a pretty special relationship."

He slapped Jonah on the shoulder. "I gotta go, man. Good luck later on. We're going all the way to the state championships this year!" He said it loud, so everyone around him could hear.

Jonah's face flushed as he waved him off and continued toward the gym.

∞

Jonah walked out onto the court with his four teammates and shook hands with the opposing team's center. But he couldn't help but be distracted by all the activity going on around him. Things only he could see, that he'd noticed as people began filing into the gym and while they were warming up.

Jonah knew he should be focusing on the court, but he spent most of the warm-up looking up.

One of his teammates standing beside him in the layup line began to look up too. "What are you looking at, man?"

"Oh," Jonah said, realizing he'd been staring. "Just stretching my neck. It's a little tight."

The kid eyed him. "Okay, whatever," he said, sounding unconvinced.

A swarm of fallen angels were in the room, dipping, whirling, and causing mayhem in the crowd. The Peacefield High fans and those from the other school were already jeering at one another, and the game hadn't even tipped off.

As Jonah stood at the center jump circle and the referee held the ball aloft, he couldn't help but look past it, into the rafters. A row full of griffins, those half-lion, half-eagle creatures, sat like giant pigeons on a telephone wire on one of the ducts. They gnashed their beaks at one another and flexed their claws.

He knew what they were there for and what they wanted. He had seen what they could do.

Jonah forgot to jump when the referee threw the ball.

"Jonah!" the coach screamed at him, jumping up and slamming his feet down together. "You awake out there?"

Jonah shook his head and tried to recover on defense, but the other team had already scored.

"Sorry, guys," he mumbled to his team, telling himself to focus.

But the fallen angels had noticed his distraction, and they were making the most of it. Jonah got the ball at the top of the circle, faked out his defender, and drove to the basket. Swooping in from his left and right, though, were two fallen angels, screaming at him.

"Don't miss, Jonah!" they jeered. "Don't miss!"

He launched himself awkwardly, the ball in his right hand.

But he swatted at the air with his left in mid-stride. Jonah landed, and the referee blew the whistle.

"Traveling!" the man in the striped shirt said as Jonah stood, looking upward again. He was only half aware of the game going on around him anymore.

"Son," the referee said. "Ball."

Jonah couldn't hear him, watching a fallen angel fly right above his head, glaring at him.

The referee blew the whistle and raised his hands into a T. "Technical foul, number thirty-four. Delay of game!" He walked over and snatched the ball from Jonah's hand.

"Huh?" Jonah said, shaking his head and pointing his thumb into his chest. "On me?"

The ref rolled his eyes.

"Stone!" Coach Marty called out. "Get over here. Now!"

Jonah trotted over to the sideline.

"Where are you today, son?" his coach said, looking up at his star player. Then he pointed to the last spot on the bench. "Why don't you take a seat over there and figure out if you want to play for us tonight or not. Okay?"

"Yes, Coach," Jonah said sheepishly, his mind still in a fog.

When the second quarter started, with his team already down by eleven points, Coach Marty called Jonah over to him. "You ready now?"

Jonah nodded. "I'm ready."

He joined the others on the court, determined to make up for his embarrassing mistakes. The crowd cheered when he stepped out, and he waved to them.

"We want to see a dunk!" a kid screamed.

"Come on, Jonah! You can do it!" another yelled.

He felt their enthusiasm fuel him, and he clapped his hands together. It was time to show them the real Jonah Stone.

His teammate threw the ball in, and instead of letting their point guard get it, Jonah stepped in front of him and grabbed the ball. Dribbling with a new level of intensity, he summoned a bit of his angelic abilities and sped by the defender as if he were standing in cement. He jumped, just inside the free throw line, and sailing through the air, threw down a monstrous one-handed dunk.

The crowd stood on its feet, screaming and jumping up and down. Jonah raised his hands in the air, beckoning them to cheer louder. He barely noticed the fallen angel sitting up in the rafters beside the griffins.

The fallen one spoke a word to the winged creatures, and suddenly they descended onto the court. Jonah was running back to play defense when he saw them come.

Ignore it, Jonah.

But they sped downward, reaching their talons out to him. Five of them were directly overhead, and then suddenly they surrounded him. He couldn't see anything.

"Get out of the way!" he said, swinging his arm out at them. "Go back to where you came from!"

"Are you okay?" he heard the voice of one of his teammates from behind, but he couldn't see him, his vision blocked by the griffins. They were screeching loudly now, though, and he instinctively brought his hands up to cover his ears, and he squeezed his eyes shut.

"Stop it!" he shouted. "Get away from me!"

In unison, they flapped their wings and retreated upward. In seconds, they were back on their perch above.

It took Jonah a moment to realize that he was standing at center court, all alone. The game around him had stopped. The gym was silent. The referees were so stunned they hadn't thought to blow a whistle.

All eyes were on him.

Jonah saw a fallen angel hover just out of his reach, smiling, enjoying the sight of the quarterling embarrassed in front of his entire school.

Before anyone could say anything, Jonah ducked his head and ran off the court, bursting through the double doors of the gym that led outside.

THIRTEEN

BUS STOP

Jonah ran to his mountain bike and fumbled with the lock, almost completely out of breath. He took a couple of seconds, hands on his knees, to gasp for air. What had happened back there? How could he have let the fallen angels get to him like that? His mind was clearing, and serious embarrassment was setting in. Jonah banged his head on his bike seat as he crouched in the dark.

"Ugh," he mumbled. He put his hands over his ears . . . how was he ever going to face his friends again?

"Jonah! Jonah?" Tariq called out through the darkness.

"Leave me alone, Tariq," he said flatly, unlocking his bike and pulling it out of the rack.

His friend walked toward him, concern etched across his face. "Look, man, I don't know what happened back there. It was like you snapped or something. What's going on with you?"

Jonah slammed his front tire down into the gravel and hopped onto the bike. "I said, *leave me alone!*" He put his foot on the pedal but didn't move. "I'm sorry, okay. I don't know what to tell you. I mean, I could tell you, but you would think I was crazy." He mumbled this last part almost to himself.

"Are you sick or something?" asked Tariq, trying to come up with ideas. "Maybe you need to go see the doctor—"

"That's not it," Jonah interrupted. "I'm not . . . sick." How could he explain this to his friend? He wanted to. He had never wanted to share something with someone so badly in this moment, so that at least another person here would know what he was dealing with. All of the past months of silence were catching up to him. He and his dad weren't talking, and he couldn't really talk to Eliza or any of the other quarterlings back in New York.

So he hadn't spoken to anyone.

Not even Elohim, he reminded himself.

"Well, whatever it was, you know that all that stuff in there"— Tariq pointed back to the gym—"that was kind of . . . weird, right? Look, I just wanted to make sure you're okay."

Jonah pushed down on the pedal of the bike and rolled past his friend. "I'm fine. Thanks, okay? I just need to sort some things out, that's all." He tried to manage a smile as he looked back. "I'll catch you tomorrow, all right?"

Tariq wrinkled his brow, waving to him slowly. "Yeah, okay."

The sky was cloud-covered as he rode home, the streets in utter darkness except for the street lamps here and there. He replayed the scene in the gym over and over in his mind, but couldn't shake it.

I can't really get away, can I?

His legs began to pedal faster and faster until he was moving at a high rate of speed past men and women in cars, driving home from work. He didn't care if they saw him move at blazing speed or not. Soon, he was wheeling into his driveway and throwing his bike into the grass.

An urge, strong and pressing, moved within him. He knew what he had to do.

"What are you doing, Jonah?"

He spun around as he grasped the door handle. The angel was standing right behind him. Her hair fell across her shoulders, black as night, but her eyes sparkled blue with flecks of silver. "You scared me, Cassandra! Man," he said, catching his breath. "Haven't I told you to never sneak up on me like that?"

She stood, a smirk on her face. "You didn't answer my question."

Jonah turned toward his guardian angel. "I'm going home. What does it look like?"

She leaned against the wooden porch post. "You really expect me to believe that? Come on, I know what's going on. Probably more than you think."

"Do you really?" Jonah demanded. "Then where have you been? Have you seen what's happening in the school? There are fallen angels all over the place and their creatures, doing all sorts of awful things to the students. And where are you? Where are the angels?"

He paused, trying to bite his tongue.

She nodded. "Go on . . . you were going to finish with 'where is Elohim?' weren't you?"

Jonah rolled his eyes. "As a matter of fact, I was." He shrugged his shoulders.

She spoke quietly. "There is a plan, and even though you cannot see it, it doesn't mean that—"

"Save it, okay? I'm tired of hearing about plans. You keep going ahead with all the plans you want. As long as they don't involve me."

Jonah slammed the door in her face and then stomped into the house.

He passed by his father's closed study. The lights were shining underneath the door. Jonah knew that he and his dad were supposed to talk tonight, but Jonah didn't want to stop and talk. His mind was made up.

Jonah vaulted the steps four at a time up to his room, changed clothes, and grabbed what he needed. In less than a minute, he was back on his bike, pedaling away from his father, Cassandra, school, his house, and everything else.

∽

Jonah stood in front of the bus terminal departure board, studying the outbound schedule, looking for whatever would take him farthest away. He had one hundred and three dollars. It was all he had left from the money he had saved mowing grass for neighbors during the summer.

"Anything far away," he muttered. Running his finger along the bus chart, one town jumped out. "Buffalo. Hmmm."

All he remembered about Buffalo was that it was near Niagara Falls, and that they had taken a trip there when he was six. He had a picture of his mom and him standing underneath the giant falls in long, black ponchos and flip-flops, soaking wet with huge grins on their faces.

That was all the encouragement he needed.

"One ticket to take me to Buffalo, New York, please," he told the bus station attendant behind the desk.

The woman glanced at him and then at the schedule. "Sixty-three dollars, please. That bus leaves at seven twenty-two. It's boarding."

Jonah handed her the money and checked the clock behind

her. That was in fifteen minutes. She gave him his ticket, and he walked outside and found the bus, ready and waiting.

He took a seat about halfway back, dropped his backpack at his feet, and settled in, trying to clear his mind. He plugged his headphones into his ears and turned on some music.

A woman, holding a duffel bag in one hand and the hand of a young girl in the other, struggled down the aisle. She arrived at the two seats across from Jonah, sighing loudly.

"Anita, get in," she said wearily. Opening the top compartment, she hefted the bag up and shoved it in. The girl, maybe two years old, stood instead, watching Jonah. He met her bright, brown eyes with his and gave her a small wave. She smiled but hid her face behind the seat.

"I said get in!" her mother scolded, pulling the girl into the seat beside her.

Another woman eased herself down the middle of the bus. She wore a rain hat and a brightly colored jacket, and carried a large brown bag. Around her neck hung a huge silver cross.

The woman stopped in front of Jonah and stared directly at him for a few seconds longer than most normally would. A look of surprise crossed her face, and she seemed to want to say something but didn't. Jonah glanced away and then looked at her again, uncomfortable with her stare. She shook her head and moved past.

When the bus was a little more than half full, the door closed and the driver picked up the microphone.

"Ladies and gentlemen, thank you for riding Greyhound buses with us this evening. Drive time to Buffalo will be approximately seven hours, with three stops along the way. Sit back and enjoy the ride."

Jonah's eyes must have closed at some point, lulled to sleep by the bus motor and the cushioned seat. But when a loud clap echoed through the bus, his eyes snapped open.

The little girl began to whimper softly. He saw a flash and heard the clap again, and realized they were in the middle of a storm. He tried to close his eyes again.

Boom! Boom!

This time the thunderclap was so loud that several people on the bus screamed. Jonah pulled his headphones out and leaned forward in his seat, looking around at the other passengers, who were doing the same thing. The rain was coming down so hard that he couldn't see much outside of the bus windows.

Jonah felt the bus jerk to the right. The mother in front of him put her hand over her mouth and held her baby tighter.

"It was just a gust of wind," Jonah said, trying to calm her. "I'm sure the bus driver knows how to handle stuff like this."

She nodded but said nothing, worry creasing her forehead as she rocked her daughter, who was sucking on two fingers.

Jonah felt drawn to the window again and stared for a long time, waiting for the rain to diminish and the thunderclaps to silence. But they didn't. They only got worse. People were crying out and screaming whenever the bus got pushed by the strong wind.

He felt someone lean forward behind him, someone's head, leaning in.

"You know, I think you'd better leave."

Jonah turned to see the old woman with the cross, sitting on her knees behind him. She had a worried look on her face.

"Excuse me?" Jonah said, wondering why someone would say such a crazy thing like this on a bus.

She tapped him on the arm. "I said, I think you'd better leave. And I mean it. You're the cause of all this."

He shook his head at her curiously. "Okay, lady."

Turning back around, he put his earphones back in, trying to ignore both the storm and the strange lady behind him.

The bus driver had slowed down but was still forging ahead on the rain-soaked road. Jonah could just make out the edge of a ravine outside of the window during the flashes of lightning. *We're getting into the hills, and it's only getting worse.* It was not a good road to be on in that weather.

Another flash of lightning and the immediate thunderclap behind it emboldened the lady behind him again.

"You, boy!" she called out. "Turn around here!"

Jonah heard her, through his music, and reluctantly sat up in his chair and turned.

It was the look in her eyes that caught him off guard—not hateful, not angry, just intensely focused. "I can see things. Things that most others in here can't," she said with a wave of her hand. "I've done it all my life, and let me tell you, I've never felt so strongly about anything as I do right now—*you need to get off this bus!*"

Suddenly, the bus tilted sharply, and the lights went out.

"Aaaahhh!" Jonah was thrown onto the floor with the other riders. The mother was shaking now, and the girl was looking at him and screaming.

The woman's words rang in his head as he watched the girl cry.

"It's okay, everybody," the bus driver's voice crackled over the loudspeaker. "Just hit a pothole in the road, nothing to worry about. Please remain calm. We should be outta this mess soon." He sounded shaky and nervous, though, and nothing he said seemed to calm anyone down a bit. And if possible, as soon as he set the microphone down and continued driving ahead, the storm grew even fiercer.

She's right.

The voice spoke deep within him. He couldn't make sense of it and couldn't explain it either, but somehow he knew that she was right.

"It's going to be okay," Jonah said to the little girl, still eyeing him as she wailed. "Don't cry. It's going to be all right."

He pulled himself up on the back of the chair in front of him and made his way to the front of the bus.

"I need to get off," Jonah said, standing beside the bus driver. The driver didn't take his eyes off the road or his hands from the wheel.

"You and everybody else," he said, smirking.

Jonah tapped him on the shoulder. "No, really, you don't understand. I need to get off, now!"

"Son," he said firmly, "don't ever touch me while I'm driving! Especially not while I'm in this storm! That clear?"

"Yes, sir," answered Jonah, taking a step back. "But really, I have to get off this bus. It will do everyone on here good if I do . . ."

"You sick?" the man asked.

Jonah ran his fingers through his tangled hair. "Well, no. I'm not sick. It's just that—"

"Then go back to your seat, son—now!" he said, raising his voice. "You're putting everyone on this bus in danger by being up here!"

Jonah exploded, "I'm putting everyone in danger by being on here at all!"

Just then, a huge bolt of lightning struck in front of them, followed immediately by a clap of thunder. Water shot at the bus as if a giant hose were spraying them, and for a minute, Jonah couldn't see out of the windshield, even though the wipers were going.

"Hold on!" the driver shouted, gripping the wheel tighter.

When the wipers swished away the water, Jonah finally saw what the lightning had hit. A towering tree was falling out of a grove in front of them. Things began to move as if in slow motion.

The tree crashed in front of the bus, fifty yards ahead. It bounced on the road once and then landed. It may as well have been a brick wall in front of them.

"Look out!" Jonah shouted.

The driver did the only thing he could do. He pushed down on the brakes, hard. But the bus started to skid immediately. Jonah grabbed the rail tightly as he felt the bus turn to the left, and as quickly as that, they were moving sideways, toward the tree.

The back of the bus whipped around, until Jonah and the bus driver were facing the road they had just come down, and they were still spinning, heading rapidly toward the edge of the road.

It seemed that everyone was screaming now, except for Jonah and the driver. But in that moment, the cries grew a little more distant in his mind. Something else pushed its way to the surface. A strange calm overcame him. Maybe there was something he could do, before they were all sent down the hillside.

The bus slid, and it was, indeed, fast coming closer to the edge. The headlights were pointing out, off the left side of the road illuminating nothing but air.

The front of the bus slid to the edge of the road as the brakes screeched, trying to stop a massive amount of metal and steel. It was slowing, but not fast enough.

Then it slowly slid beyond the edge.

The driver held on to the steering wheel, but the front two tires were hanging off the road. He held on to the wheel and stared straight ahead, apparently in shock.

"To the back of the bus!" Jonah shouted, helping the people

sitting at the front get up and move toward the back. "Everybody! Get up and go to the back, fast!"

They snapped to attention and scrambled to the rear as fast as they could.

"Come on, sir!" Jonah said to the driver. He pushed him on the arm. "We have to get to the back, now!"

He reached over and unbuckled the man's seat belt for him, which seemed to wake him from the shock. He nodded, mumbling something, and Jonah pushed him to the back with the rest of the passengers.

The bus was still creeping forward. Jonah stood at the front for a second, unsure if he should join the others. He looked at them, then to the bank of buttons beside the steering wheel.

What am I supposed to do?

The mom of the little girl stood with her daughter, still crying, and beckoned him. "Come," she said. "Come now!"

The driver had sprung into action and was opening the rear emergency door with the help of a middle-aged man in the back.

Jonah hesitated.

"You need to get off this bus!"

The old woman's words rang one last time, and he quickly reached behind him. He found the right button and pushed it.

The front door opened, and he took a step down as he looked back at the passengers.

"What are you doing?" the mother screamed. "Come this way! Come this way!"

But the last face he saw was the older woman with the cross, who stood silently.

There was no time left, and the bus was still sliding. He summoned every ounce of strength he had and leaped.

FOURTEEN

BELOW AND ALONE

Jonah soared through the air, barely reaching the metal guard-rail with his left hand. He grabbed on as tightly as he could. The bus had already ripped through it, but it held him, for now. With his right hand, he grabbed the luggage compartment handle on the bus and flipped it up. Bags spilled out from underneath, hurtling into the darkness below. He grabbed the solid inside of the compartment and held it with all his might.

He looked up as his arms were outstretched, one on the guardrail, the other on the bus, holding them there with every-thing he had. Through the window just above him, he thought he saw the faint outline of the little girl's face, pointing to him and saying something to her mother.

"Aaaaaaaaggggghhhhh!" he cried out. He was barely alert enough to realize that it had stopped raining. And no more thun-der or lightning. "Get off, people," he whispered. "Please, get off, so I can let go . . ."

Please, Elohim, let me . . .

Jonah pushed as hard as he could, and the bus began to move very slowly back up onto the road. He continued, feeling it move a little more with each shove.

The open front door was almost within reach when he heard shouts up above.

"We're out! Hey, we're out, kid! Get back up here! Everyone's safe! Everyone's safe!"

He felt a jolt of energy and gave the bus one last shove, knowing what he had to do. Reaching the doorway again, he pulled himself back inside the bus. He was alone on it, which he was thankful for. They really had gotten off. He hurried toward the back. Outside the windows, he saw the passengers lined up, some of whom were waving to him to jump through the emergency exit and onto safe ground.

He was almost there when he realized he wasn't going to make it.

The bus began to slip again. He ran for the exit, but before he could get there, it fell right over the edge, taking Jonah with it.

Jonah felt himself falling backward. His head hit something hard, and then he saw nothing but black.

∽

Jonah heard a distant, creaking sound, and at first, he couldn't open his eyes. *Where am I?* He tried to sort through memories, but they were jumbled. Images of his mom flashed through his mind, another of him holding a blazing sword on a dark street, a black-haired girl smiling at him, his brother looking down at him from the top bunk . . . a clutter of snapshots danced in front of him, and for a while he struggled to find where he was.

His head hurt more than it ever had before. The smell of smoke, oil, and electricity filled his nose, and it helped him crack his eyes open. The strange sight above confused him. A faint light poured around him, and he was able to make out chairs . . . on the ceiling. He blinked at them for at least a minute, trying to place them.

Then the memories fell together like tumblers in a lock. The basketball game . . . his conversation with Cassandra . . . the face of a little girl . . . a bus ride . . . the storm . . . and the fall from the road, high above. He realized he was sprawled out on the ceiling of the inside of the bus, which was now upside down.

Slowly, he pushed himself up off the cold metal until he was sitting. His entire body ached, but as he examined his arms and legs, as far as he could tell, nothing was broken. He took another few minutes and then gingerly tried to stand. He knew he had to get out of the bus.

Ducking his head low, he felt a crunching beneath his feet and realized he was stepping on broken shards of glass. The windows had been smashed, and the openings that had been there weren't anymore.

I'll try the front door, he thought.

But when he arrived at the front of the bus, he saw that the glass in the door had been broken out too, and the metal was mangled shut. It was hard to see, but it also seemed as though the bus was resting up against a wall of rock. There would be no getting out through the door.

Frantically, he began to look around for any opening, any crack that he could force his body through. But the windshield was smashed too, crimped down with no opening. He searched the entire bus, but there was no way out.

He was trapped.

"I'm like dog food trapped in a can," he muttered. Then he began to yell, "Help! Help me! I'm trapped in here!"

Jonah listened for a few seconds. All he heard was the wind whistling through the trees and the sound of running water rushing by. There were no signs of help, apparently no search team, and nobody calling his name.

Then reality hit him.

He was all alone.

cMo

Jonah had no idea how much time had passed. Ten minutes. Or ten hours . . . he didn't know. He was sitting, absorbed in his own thoughts, trying to figure out how he had gotten himself into this awful mess. Was the accident really his fault? It had stopped raining as soon as he got off the bus. The lightning and thunder had stopped too. Not gradually. Immediately.

But then he must have fallen asleep for a while. He felt disoriented, trying to make the scene in front of him fit with where his brain was.

He'd been dreaming again. He saw Jeremiah, just as he had in the mirror back at school. He was still alone, but instead of searching for something, he seemed to be running. Someone, or something, was chasing him.

He had a look of fear on his face that Jonah had never seen before. Jonah was trying, somehow, in his dream, to help him. To reach out to him and let him know it was okay. But just as he was about to get there, he had woken up.

Jonah slammed his hand down on the floor of the bus, which

was really the ceiling, in frustration. As he did, he noticed his backpack bounce behind him, against the side of the bus. His phone fell out. The notification signal was blinking red.

Jonah!

I hope you get this soon! Jeremiah's been taken! He's gone. I was chasing after him, trying to find him, because he went looking for Mom. He thought he saw her on the street. I know this doesn't make any sense. I will explain. Just come . . . or call me . . . or something!

He needs you. And so do I! Please, Jonah . . .

FIFTEEN

CAMILLA AND THE COPS

Eliza had called as many people as she could as she ran home, trying to wake them up and alert them to the fact that Jeremiah was gone. It was still early, though, and the only person she'd been able to get on the phone was Julia, who had her phone on her bedside table.

"You need to call the police, Eliza!" she said, sitting straight up in bed.

Eliza was running as fast as she could, with barely enough breath to talk. "I want to tell Camilla first and see what she wants to do, Julia. I just can't believe . . . I just can't believe . . ."

"It's okay," said Julia, trying to be as reassuring as she could. "We'll find him."

Eliza could hear the strain in her voice, though, and all of the unsaid words strung through her mind. *What if they didn't find him, though? What if they couldn't? How would they know where he went and who had taken him?*

What if they never saw him again?

And it was all happening under her watch.

She felt the weight of her failed responsibilities crashing down upon her. Her shoulders drooped as she pressed on, feet slapping the cold concrete. She was supposed to protect her brother. That's what her mom would've wanted her to do.

Camilla was waiting for her at the door of the convent with Julia.

As soon as Eliza saw them, she burst into tears.

"Oh, dear, come here!" the angel said, wrapping her arms around Eliza tightly.

"I didn't mean to lose him," she said, her words muffled. "I tried . . ."

"It's Jeremiah," Camilla said. "He's hard to keep up with. But let's go to my office now. You need to tell me everything you know."

Eliza sat in her office with Julia, recounting everything with as much detail as she could remember, from Jeremiah's description of seeing Eleanor, to everything she could remember about the men with Jeremiah, to the car they put him in. Sister Patricia entered the office quietly at some point and stood waiting at the door.

"Sister Patricia," Camilla said. "You will call the police immediately and report Jeremiah as having been kidnapped. We need all the resources we can get to find him."

She nodded and stepped out of the office.

Camilla stood. "I will gather the rest together, and we will search for him, alerting the Second Battalion of the Angelic Forces of the West to help. Don't worry, Eliza," she said, patting Eliza on the shoulder as she hurried past. "He can't have gotten very far."

Eliza followed her out into the hallway, where they found all of the quarterlings standing and waiting. Even though it was early, they were all dressed and had somber looks on their faces.

"Excellent, you are all ready then," said Camilla. "Step into the dining hall for a moment, and we will get organized!"

Eliza felt her eyes well up again when she saw the others, ready to help and encourage her.

"We'll find him."

"Don't worry, Eliza. He can't be very far away."

"Jeremiah is tough. He won't let them get away with anything."

A hand eased around her shoulder. "We're going to get him back," Frederick said, winking at her and offering a smile. "Remember, it's Jeremiah—by the time he talks their ears off for fifteen minutes, they'll probably throw him out of the car and be on their way."

She didn't laugh but rested her head on his shoulder for a second. "Thank you. Thanks to all of you for being willing to help."

Everyone loved Jeremiah. He was almost like their group mascot, and she was grateful that they both had such wonderful friends.

Camilla organized them into search parties, instructing them to go out at once and scour the area around the factory, moving gradually away from it.

"Remember, we are looking for a black four-door sedan with two men and Jeremiah. I know there are a lot of those cars in this city, but with the help of Elohim, we will no doubt find him," Marcus instructed.

His confidence inspired the quarterlings, and they were itching to hit the streets with their teams.

"Eliza," Sister Patricia said, sticking her head just inside the door. "The police are here."

She walked into the hallway and past the prayer room, which was full of nuns already on their knees, calling out to Elohim. She heard Jeremiah's name over and over, and she knew that if she were in the hidden realm, she would see tendrils of light joining those that were praying together and pouring as one upward.

Two police officers stood in the doorway, along with a woman dressed in a sharp-fitting navy suit. They were speaking with a couple of the nuns as Eliza walked up.

"Eliza," the woman said, extending her hand and looking at her seriously. "I'm Officer Kelly, and I'm sorry to hear about your brother. These are officers Anderson and Reilly. We'd like to know as much as you can tell us about what happened."

They sat down in some chairs in the lobby, and Eliza took a deep breath to tell the story again. But she hesitated before launching in. What could she tell them about their first visit down to the factory? About Jeremiah thinking he saw his mom? About the attacks? She couldn't just come out and say, "Well, we were being attacked by fallen angels because my brother thought he saw our dead mother, so we had to escape, and we jumped into a moving truck." She silently prayed that she would be able to figure out a way to tell the story without lying.

Officer Kelly asked her to detail exactly what happened, and Eliza offered everything she could think of. She spent most of the time trying to describe as much as she could about the men she saw take Jeremiah. She'd seen them for only a second or two at the most, but she could remember certain things. One had curly gray hair, and the other was wearing a black stocking cap. Both had black trench coats on. She had seen one shoe, worn by the gray-haired man—a light brown boot.

Kelly was impressed. "You have a remarkable memory, Eliza," she said, making notes in a spiral-bound notebook resting on her knee. "So tell me what you saw the first time you two were there that made him want to come back."

"Well, I was looking for him, because he had wandered off, which Jeremiah is prone to do," she said. "He thought he'd seen our mother. She . . . passed away last year."

Kelly glanced up from her notes and blinked. "I'm so sorry, Eliza."

Eliza continued, "We ended up going into this factory by accident. We got out by going downstairs into the parking deck."

She decided to skip the part about riding in the yellow truck.

Officer Kelly chewed on her pen for a minute and seemed to want to say something else, but then closed her notebook. "We're going to put as many people as we can on this. Hopefully we can have some news for you soon." She looked around the hallway for a minute. "What kind of school is this again?"

"It's a Christian boarding school for international students," Eliza answered, hoping that answer would satisfy her. Kelly shrugged and handed Eliza her card. "Call me if you think of anything else. I'll be back in touch."

She turned to go with the other two officers. Eliza wondered how much help they would really be, but then she remembered that they were looking for real people and vehicles in the physical world, and the more help, the better.

Eliza stepped into the prayer room, sinking to her knees beside the women already praying. Silently, she entered the hidden realm, watching for a few seconds as the white glowing ropes moved through them and into the ceiling, alive, pulsating, coming from the heartfelt prayers that were being offered.

"Elohim," she whispered. "Please, if You will, please let us find my little brother. Please help guide us in the right direction. I know You have a plan. You have a purpose in all of this. Nothing happens without You knowing about it first. Whatever happens, I want to ask that he please be returned safely here. Let him know that You're with him right now."

She stayed another minute, listening to the others pray. Then quietly she stood, throwing up one more quick prayer.

"Please . . . the last thing our family needs is to lose someone else."

SIXTEEN

IN THE RAVINE

J onah sat up on his knees.

"Help!" he screamed as loudly as his lungs could handle. "Help! Someone get me out of here!"

He pushed against the walls as hard as he could. With all his angel strength, he pushed. But the sides wouldn't budge. He couldn't move them. He tried, again and again, hitting them with his fists, karate chopping them with his feet. It was like they were made of something quarterling resistant.

Eliza's text had caused something to break within him. All of his pretending, all the hiding, the running, and the acting as if he were someone that he wasn't. All of it was stripped bare in the moment he realized his brother was in trouble and his sister needed him and he couldn't do anything to help. He had neglected them, he had turned his back on them, and he knew it. He had let his anger and despair affect not only him but his family.

Now they were in trouble, and he was on the other side of the world—at least it felt like that—so far away that he couldn't do anything.

"I can't do anything for anyone," he muttered. "I'm stuck here in this bus."

Another reality hit him just as hard, and just as fast, in the darkness of the prison he was in. Eliza and Jeremiah, and his father, for that matter, weren't the only ones he had neglected.

He fell again to his knees.

"Elohim," he whispered. Over and over, the name came from his lips, His name the only sound there in the night.

"I'm done," Jonah cried out. "I can't do this anymore. Not on my own. You called to me, and I ran away. I tried to do everything on my own, everything. You chased after me, but I wouldn't listen. You told me to go to New York, back with Eliza and Jeremiah . . . You told me to treat my dad differently than I have. And I didn't do any of it. And look where I am. Right here, trapped in this bus at the bottom of a cliff."

The tears rose in waves, and he let them come. His chest heaved, and an image of his mother's face sprang across his mind.

"Mom . . . ," he said, when his breathing finally slowed again. "I've been so upset, so mad about it all. You took her away, and I don't get it. I don't. But how I've been dealing with things, well, it obviously hasn't helped. I don't know what to do about all of that, about how much I miss her." He stopped for a minute to gather his thoughts. "But I know that running from You isn't the answer. I only ended up running from who I am, not running from You."

Jonah lay down on the floor. "I'm ready to go, Elohim," he finally said. "Ready to do whatever it is You want me to do."

He fell asleep again, his head resting against a cushion, which was covered with his tears.

c√っ

He awoke to a light shining down from the sky, illuminating the trees outside.

"Is that You?" Jonah asked sleepily, picking himself up from the floor.

He heard voices, faint at first, but growing louder. They were shouting, and soon he could make out the words.

"Hey! Is anyone down there? Anyone alive?"

Jonah moved close to the side where he could see through a small crack the size of a basketball. He could hear a whirring sound and saw a couple of ropes dangling in a clearing beside the wreckage he was in.

Several men were sliding down on ropes, which were attached to a helicopter, floating just above the tree line.

"I'm here! Yes!" he shouted. "I'm in here!"

The rescue didn't take very long. Within minutes, the search-and-rescue team had cut through the side of the bus with their special tools, cracking it open like a coconut. Then they pulled Jonah back up to the road in a harness.

As Jonah sat with the medics a few minutes later, back at the top of the cliff, he could finally see where he had fallen.

"Son, you are one lucky kid," said the man placing bandages on a couple of scrapes on his arms and legs. He nodded in the direction of the cliff. "Never seen anyone go over anything like that before. And I've definitely never seen anyone come out alive. Somebody's watching out for you."

Jonah nodded, and he knew that luck had nothing to do with it. And yes, more than ever, he was convinced that someone was indeed watching out for him.

PART III

CONFRONTATIONS

What I have vowed I will make good. I will

say, "Salvation comes from the LORD."

Jonah 2:9 NIV

SEVENTEEN

THE UN

"Y es," Vitaly Cherkov said to his assistant as they strode down the marble hallway, expensive leather shoes clicking along at a fast pace. He nodded to another ambassador passing in the other direction with his entourage surrounding him. The halls of the United Nations building in New York City were sacred ground to most who served there. They were a symbol of the efforts of the world to bring unity and peace, to hammer out disagreements in a civilized manner—a triumph of freedom over tyranny.

To Vitaly, though, all of this was old news from another era. He had been here a long, long time, and he knew how things really worked. There were people of passion, sacrifice, and service here, to be sure. But most of them were much younger than he and still had the audacity to think they could change the world with a little bit of effort and diplomacy. Vitaly played the game well, but experience and time had taught him differently.

His mind wandered back to last night. The visit from the special aide to the United Nations had been unexpected, and at first, unwanted. But what he had seen in the man's eyes had startled him. He had spent the next two hours lying in his bed, unable to go to sleep—craving what he'd seen. His hands had trembled so much he'd had to push them underneath his pillow to get them to stop.

He was having trouble remembering the specifics, though. But he did know that he had seen himself in the future. And one thing was for sure—he was sitting on a throne.

When he finally dozed off for a fitful hour of sleep, he had awful, unspeakable nightmares.

In these morning hours, though, his rational side was kicking in. He would not be bought, let alone intimidated by this, or any, mere man. He had to be strong. The vision must have been some strange hallucination. Perhaps a bad batch of caviar he'd tasted the night before was responsible.

"Sir, you have approximately three minutes until your morning briefing," his aide said, walking a pace ahead as he glanced at his watch. Another young man helped him slide out of his overcoat, revealing an expensive Italian suit. "We don't want to be late."

He glared at his aide. "Yes, yes," was all he said, taking the folder from him and glancing through it.

Mr. Prince was sitting on a bench in the hallway when they rounded the corner, sipping coffee out of a Styrofoam cup. Vitaly saw him and dropped the folder onto the floor.

"Watch that," Mr. Prince called out, sipping again. "Don't want to get any of those important files mixed up." He chuckled.

Vitaly felt his hands trembling again and shoved them in his pockets. He tried not to acknowledge the comment, walking past the man on the bench as his aide picked up the file.

"A minute of your time, if you please, sir," Mr. Prince called out as Vitaly walked past.

Vitaly hesitated, closing his eyes for a few seconds, but not turning back.

His aide cut a glance toward Mr. Prince. "He is about to be late for a meeting, sir," he said, continuing to walk ahead.

"It's okay. I won't be long," Mr. Prince said, standing up. "You can make a few minutes for me, can't you, Vitaly?"

Vitaly turned around, his mind back on the strange vision. "A few minutes, of course."

"But, sir, we're going to be—"

"It's okay, Sergey!" he said, his voice rising. "It will only be a minute, no longer."

"What is it you want?" Vitaly hissed quietly. "He is right. I have an important meeting today."

Mr. Prince walked slowly, as if he had all the time in the world. "Now, Vitaly, you take that tone with me, after all I shared with you last night?" he said, placing his hand on his shoulder.

Vitaly felt the weight of his grasp, although he couldn't tell if the man was squeezing hard or if his arm just felt extraordinarily heavy. Another contingent of diplomats walked briskly by, and he managed to give them a nod and a strained smile as they greeted him.

When they were alone again, he turned to Mr. Prince. "I am going to be late. But, yes, last night was quite . . . impressive."

"I know you are a busy man," Mr. Prince said, eyes gleaming, "and I certainly don't want to take up too much of your time. I hope you had some wonderful dreams last night."

Vitaly glared at him. If he only knew the awful nightmares he'd had. "Yes, yes, I did."

Prince grinned. "Just remember, I only gave you a taste last night of what's to come. There is more. Much more."

He took a sip from the white cup, allowing his words to sink in.

Vitaly couldn't help it. He longed to look into the man's eyes again. "More, you say?"

Mr. Prince smiled, nodding. "That is what I'll do for you, Vitaly. You have to trust me. But today, I need something from you."

Vitaly twitched, pushing his shaking hands into his pockets again. There was something about talking to this man. No one in the meeting room full of important people he was about to enter made him feel quite this nervous, and excited, all at once.

"I just want a list of names, that's all," Mr. Prince said, locking eyes with the Russian. "A list of the people attending the party on your boat tomorrow night. The celebration of the year is what I've heard. Many dignitaries will be there to honor the recent accomplishments you've made in world peace. To toast the victories you have sustained all over the world. It's been truly impressive, Vitaly. I'd like to know exactly who is going to be there."

Vitaly glanced back at his aides, who were waiting impatiently down the hall. He raised a finger to them signaling one more minute. "Why do you need such a list?"

"Why I need it is not really anything you need to know," he said. "I just need to know if you're going to do this for me. Otherwise . . ."

He let the word linger, and Vitaly thought of the consequences of losing the trust of this man—what he'd seen would never become reality.

"Fine, fine," he said. "I will get you the list. But that's all, is that clear?"

Mr. Prince laughed, and then drew very close to him so that Vitaly could see his yellowing teeth and smell his rancid breath. Prince squeezed his arm until Vitaly thought his bones might crack. "It will be *all* when I say it's *all*, Mr. Ambassador. Is *that* clear?"

Vitaly felt the pain shoot through his arm, and, trying not to squeal, he nodded silently.

Mr. Prince straightened the ambassador's jacket, his tone soothing once again. "Otherwise, things may not happen for you like they're supposed to. Like I want them to."

"Is everything all right, Mr. Ambassador?" Sergey, Vitaly's aide, asked, walking toward them slowly.

Vitaly checked his tie. "Yes, everything is fine. Let's go," he said. He nodded to the man. "Mr. Prince."

Mr. Prince tipped his cap to the ambassador and winked at Sergey.

"And now we are very late!" Sergey fretted. "What was all of that?"

"None of your business!" Vitaly snapped, and then waved his hand at his assistant. "I'm sorry, Sergey. It was nothing. My notes, please."

Sergey handed him the folder, studying his boss.

They were about to walk into the meeting room when Vitaly stopped, turning to his trusted aide. "One more thing. I need a copy of the attendance list for the party."

Sergey eyed him narrowly. "Sir, you know that lists like that are not something we hand out to people, even someone like Mr. Prince."

"It's not for him!" Vitaly declared. "Just get me a copy of the list. All right? That is all."

He nodded, dismissing his assistant as he closed the door behind him. Sergey stood in the hall for a few seconds, debating. Then he turned and scurried away, his leather shoes slapping furiously on the marble.

EIGHTEEN

SEARCHING THE STREETS

All of the quarterlings had arrived at the street where Jeremiah was taken as fast as they could. They had agreed to move in different directions, staying in touch with each other through their cell phones. They would text one another if they saw something suspicious.

Eliza hurried to catch up with her team, who had already begun the search while she spoke to the police. She noticed the angels overhead, flying slowly, dipping down every once in a while to check something out. They were looking for him too, which was at least a little bit comforting.

Her stomach wrenched, though, as she thought about Jeremiah and what he might be going through. Was he safe? Where had they taken him? Who were these people? She tried to focus on the task at hand, but that was nearly impossible. She walked even faster, keeping her eyes alert for a black car or a yellow truck.

There was one big problem with that strategy—practically every car that passed was a black sedan. Each time one of them came her direction, she tried to see in the windows. Most of the time she couldn't see anything through tinted windows, but sometimes she caught a glimpse of a face or some eyes. *Is that him?* she found herself thinking with every passing car.

Finally she caught up with Frederick, Andre, and Rupert. Rupert was staring into a black car waiting at a stoplight. The driver lowered the window and yelled something at him that sounded angry, and then sped off as the light changed.

"Sorry, then!" Rupert called out.

"Any luck so far?" Eliza asked.

"Well, there you are," he said. "No, nothing yet. Finding him in one of these black cars is going to be like finding a needle in a haystack . . ." She grimaced, and he spoke with a softer tone. "But we'll find him, Eliza. We will. Don't you worry a bit."

His less than convincing tone didn't help Eliza's stomach from doing somersaults inside.

"We have to, Rupert," she said, pushing the tears back down again. "Let's move faster."

Eliza asked Frederick and Andre to cover the other side of the street, in the hopes that they could see more cars if they split up. Traffic was starting to pick up, and they were having a tougher and tougher time scanning all of the cars.

Then she saw it—a black car, moving in their direction, with two men sitting in the front. The driver had silvery gray hair. She watched it closely as it drove past them. Yes . . . there was someone in the back, and it looked like a kid!

"There." She pointed, beginning to walk after it. "Right there! That's it! Jeremiah!"

Eliza began to run after the car. It was speeding along and quickly moving farther ahead. But she continued to run.

"Guys!" she called out to Andre and Frederick. "This way!"

They had already heard her and were heading in her direction. Frederick sped quickly past Andre, using his sandals of speed to catch up.

"You saw him?" he said, slowing down to her speed, which was still a full-on sprint.

"Right there!" she panted. "In that car, straight ahead!"

The black sedan stopped at a red light, waiting behind a yellow taxi, and to its left, a long city bus.

Eliza didn't try to sneak up on it. It was too late for caution now. Running up to the rear door, she grabbed the handle and threw it open.

"Jeremiah!" she screamed, leaning down into the car.

The driver swung his head toward her. "What in the . . . what do you think you're doing?"

She blinked at him for a few seconds, then really looked in the backseat. A neatly dressed girl was sitting there with a lunch box in her lap. She looked terrified and began to scream.

The man in the passenger seat reached back and slammed the door shut. The light had already turned green, and the car sped off, tires screeching against the pavement.

Eliza stood there for a few seconds, stunned. She had been so sure it was Jeremiah.

"You've got to be more careful, Eliza," Andre said, running up and huffing heavily in the cold air. "You could get yourself run over."

"I thought it was him," she mumbled, but quickly regained her focus. "Let's keep moving."

She texted while they walked and soon got replies from the other teams. No one had seen anything, although apparently some of them had had a few false alarms of their own.

They continued searching. One hour led to two, then to three. They were getting nowhere, although none of them, especially Eliza, wanted to admit it.

"Maybe the police are having some success," Frederick said to Eliza hopefully.

She nodded. "We'd have heard something by now, though, don't you think?"

Just then, she heard her phone sound off. Three beeps, coming from her pocket, all in a row.

Pulling it out, she pressed her glasses up on her nose.

"Three different messages," she said. "The first is from Julia . . ."

Help! Under attack!

Please hurry

Corner of Water and Hanover

Rupert already had his phone out and was plugging the street names in. "We're only a few blocks away from them!"

Eliza eyed him. "Well, you're not going to believe this, but the other two texts are from David and Hai Ling. It looks like they're all in trouble."

They looked at each other for a few seconds on the street, trying to figure out what to do.

Eliza took charge. "If they're fighting, maybe it means they've discovered something. Maybe one of them has found him!"

"I sure hope the angels are already there, doing some of the fighting too," said Andre.

Rupert determined that the closest address belonged to Julia's group.

"Let's go there first, and maybe we can help," Eliza said. She didn't even wait for the others to respond.

Rupert called out to her, panic in his voice. "Don't you think we ought to discuss this . . . perhaps take a vote?"

But she wasn't listening. She reached down to her side and pulled out her angelblade.

Eliza, Andre, Frederick, and a reluctant Rupert found Water Street and were close to the corner of Hanover when they saw the battle ahead from within the hidden realm.

"There's more going on than I thought there would be," Frederick said, watching the fallen angels fly all through the sky, firing arrows and swinging blades. Most of the battle was taking place in the air, with angels fighting back bravely. There were flashes of light and blasts of fire all over.

There was activity on the ground too, though.

"There they are!" Andre pointed, and Eliza hurried down the street, the others trailing behind.

The round glow of Julia's shield of faith shone brightly in the middle of the chaos. They could see several fallen angels hovering over it, shooting arrows into the shield. Each time they bounced off, but this didn't seem to be deterring the evil creatures from their attack. Inside the bubble, Eliza could see Lania and Carlo hunkered down beside Julia and Bridget. Both had their hands raised.

"Bridget has her shield up too," she called out to the others. "Hurry up! We need to help them!"

Lania was firing arrows through the shield and into as many fallen angels as she could. One fell just as they arrived, squirming on the ground before dissolving right in front of them.

"You got my message!" Julia cried, a faint smile on her lips.

Eliza nodded, just before launching herself at a fallen angel and swinging her blade. "Take that!" she screamed as she connected with a fallen angel, driving the blade right through his chest. He exploded into a million pieces of dust.

Rupert threw up a shield of his own, trying to protect her whenever he could catch up to her. Andre had resorted to his angelic strength, grabbing any fallen angel he could and throwing them into the wall of the building beside them. Within seconds, he had already taken out two of them.

Frederick was putting his archery skills to work. Eliza was grateful to have him by their side as she watched fallen angel after fallen angel drop from the sky.

Eliza continued to battle, clashing swords with fallen angels on the ground. One particularly nasty creature rushed at her with his blade raised high, glowing red. She blocked it with her blade, but another one was behind her and swung at the same time.

Rupert grabbed the fallen angel's arm just in time, stopping the blade from coming down inches away from her neck. Quickly, Eliza pushed off the first creature and drove her blade into his stomach. She spun and finished the second one off.

"Thanks, Rupert," she said, breathing heavily.

The sky seemed to be growing darker, and Eliza's attention was drawn upward. It wasn't from a stray cloud, though. Fallen angels were arriving by the dozens, soaring through the air above, clouding the sky. She had never seen so many in one place.

"We have to get out of here," Frederick said, watching the sky as he pulled her back.

The angels seemed to have come to the same conclusion. One of them called out to the others, "Retreat! Fall back at once!" He looked down at the quarterlings and repeated his command with force. "Retreat!"

Julia dropped her shield, and they all turned to run. Several angels flew overhead, still firing arrows, covering for them while they ran across the street and then down the block. Eliza turned to see one of them fall, a flaming arrow piercing his chest. The angel exploded into white dust, which hung in the air like snowflakes. She watched the awful, beautiful flakes glittering down softly. The fallen angels were driving toward them, firing arrows and throwing spears. Another angel fell in front of her, dropping at her feet. She watched, frozen, as the angel melted away.

"Come on, Eliza!" Rupert said, grabbing her arm and yanking it hard. It snapped her out of her daze, and she ran with the rest, determined not to look back.

After several blocks, they realized they weren't being followed anymore. They slowed down to catch their breath. A group of angels stood at the street corner, discussing the attack in hushed tones and regrouping.

"Why did they stop?" Eliza asked. One of the angels put his hand up to silence her.

She grabbed her phone from her pocket and checked it for messages. "I wonder how the others are doing," she whispered.

No messages waiting. She furiously typed in a short note to both David and Hai Ling.

We're retreating. Are you okay???

They stood in silence on the corner, watching people walk by, entirely unaware of their presence in the hidden realm.

"It just seems weird that they stopped, with that many on their side," Eliza said again, kicking at the concrete.

"Maybe they just wanted to scare us," Andre said hopefully.

She narrowed her eyes. "Do you really think that's all they want to do? After all we've been through? No, they want to kill us," she said matter-of-factly. "And they won't stop until they do."

Eliza watched her phone in silence, and Andre, Rupert, and Frederick watched her. She couldn't keep still.

"Maybe we should go find them," she said. She gestured to the angels until one came down to talk to her. "Where are the others? What's going on? Have you heard anything?"

The angel smiled kindly but was short with her. "We're working on it."

Eliza threw up her hands. "I'm going. Are you guys coming with me? We can't just stand here if they're in trouble. Maybe they have Jeremiah."

She had begun to hurry down the street when her phone beeped.

"Message!" she called out to them, studying her phone. She sighed, beginning to type a response. "They're okay. They've retreated too. I'm going to see if they've had any sign from Jeremiah."

They had waited only a few seconds this time when her phone pinged again. She frowned. "Nothing. They're heading back to the convent."

She looked down the street, in the direction they'd retreated from.

"We need to go back and get our heads together with the others," said Frederick. "I know you want to jump back in, but we need to trust that Elohim knows what He's doing here, Eliza."

She smirked. "That's funny, coming from you," she said.

He brushed off the insult. "Come on, let's go and meet with the others."

"Fine," she grumped, storming ahead in the direction of the convent.

NINETEEN

ELIZA'S HUNCH

All of the quarterlings were down in their basement lounge, resting and discussing the attacks. Each of the three groups had a surprisingly similar story. They were searching for Jeremiah, looking everywhere, when they suddenly came under attack. Angels had rushed in, offering protection where they could, but they had all been overwhelmed by a large number of fallen angels. Their only choice had been to retreat.

"It's not worth it right now," one of the angel commanders had told David. "We'll fight them another day."

Eliza grabbed a plastic cup and poured a soda from the machine. Even that made her tear up, though, as she thought about Jeremiah and how much he loved soda. Right now, she would do anything to be able to give him one.

She yanked her phone out of her pocket and found the number she wanted. The phone rang a couple of times, then rolled straight into voice mail.

She didn't even try to hide the disappointment and anger in her voice.

"Where are you, Jonah? I haven't heard back from you, haven't even gotten a text. Jeremiah is in trouble, he's been kidnapped, and I don't even know if you got that message from me or not. I don't even know if you care anymore. But if you were here—" She paused, trying to keep her voice from cracking, and composed herself. "If you were here, you would really be able to help us out. I just don't know where you are, and your own brother is missing, and I . . . I . . ." *Forget it*, she thought. She hung up.

"Hey," Julia said softly, just behind her. Eliza turned, tears streaming down her face. "It's okay, Eliza. It's going to be all right. You need to rest for a few minutes. Come sit down with us. We'll figure it out."

Eliza nodded, taking a sip of her drink and sitting on the corner of a sofa in the middle of the room.

She sighed loudly and closed her eyes. She would force herself to be quiet. She would make herself concentrate on the only one who could help them.

Elohim, she prayed, *we are stuck. I don't know where to turn now. We don't have any more clues to go on. The police don't seem to be getting anywhere, and Jeremiah is out there somewhere, lost and alone, and maybe hurt. I would do anything to get him back, absolutely anything. Maybe somehow You could switch my place with him . . .*

She sat silently, pausing, her upper lip beginning to tremble again.

Just please help us find him. Show us the way.

David put down his phone and walked over to her. "The police haven't found anything yet," he said. "They are continuing their efforts, though. They say that they're not going to stop until—"

"Well, they don't know what they're dealing with, do they?" Eliza interrupted. The whole room grew silent, everyone cutting their eyes toward her. "I mean, they hardly know what to look for, and we've all seen that finding a kid in a black car in New York City is like . . ."

She stopped in mid-sentence. A light had begun to glow in the corner of the room. It was hovering over the television.

She walked closer to it, studying the light. Elohim was trying to show her something. She could feel it.

Her eyes were drawn up to the television, which was on mute.

"Does anyone have the remote control?" she suddenly said. "Can somebody turn the volume on?"

On the screen was a man in front of a bank of microphones. Behind him were a dozen or so people, all of whom were in suits and ties, looking very official. They were standing in front of a building, where several flags from different countries could be seen waving in the sunlight.

"Why do you want to see a random news conference on CNN?" asked Rupert.

She hushed him. "Someone just turn it up, please."

The caption underneath the man read: *United Nations agrees to historic African peace treaty*

And underneath that: *Vitaly Cherkov, Russian Ambassador to the United States*

"It is my pleasure to announce that I—that we—have been able to negotiate a historic peace treaty between the countries of northern Africa, and that, largely because of the efforts of my own office, as well as the officials from both of these countries, that the millions of people there will be able to enjoy year upon year of peaceful, productive living in their countries . . ."

He continued on and on, smiling, somehow projecting humility while pulling the message back to himself and how he had accomplished great things on behalf of these countries. Behind him were representatives from several African nations. They all appeared stone-faced but nodded along as the Russian ambassador spoke.

That wasn't who Eliza was looking at, though. She stepped close to the television, looking at the men who stood behind Cherkov.

Could that be him? A man in a dark suit, with curly, silvery gray hair stood in the background. He wore sunglasses, his hands were clasped in front of him, and his head moved back and forth, as if he were watching the crowd.

Eliza pointed at the man. "It's him!" she shouted. "That guy, I know it. I'm sure of it! It's him!"

"It's who, Eliza?" Rupert asked, standing beside her and squinting at the screen.

She punched him in the arm, a little too hard. "One of the guys who took Jeremiah!"

He rubbed his arm in pain. "Are you sure? Some guy with the Russian ambassador to the United States . . . he took Jeremiah?"

"He looks like he's watching for something," Frederick observed. "I think he's security."

Hai Ling had moved over to a computer against the opposite wall and was busy clacking away.

"You want to know some information about this ambassador?" she called out to the rest. She quickly scanned several articles at once, clicking from page to page.

"Vitaly Cherkov, the Russian ambassador to the United States.

He's been in that position since 2006. He has a long history of political service, though. His entire career seems to have been in Russian politics. Apparently his uncle used to have the same position, back in the 1980s."

This news caught Andre's attention. "Yes, the Cherkovs are like kings and queens in my homeland Russia. Everyone knows who they are. They've made billions of dollars in oil . . . and probably other things that aren't quite so legal."

Hai Ling tugged at her lower lip. "I guess they have enough money to buy a mega yacht. This story is all about their giant boat, and the special permission it took to be able to dock it in New York Harbor. The thing is enormous. Look at this picture."

They oohed and aahed over the boat for a few moments. Eliza stepped back, though, her mind churning.

"Where exactly is it docked, Hai Ling?"

Hai Ling studied the article for a few more seconds, scrolling down until she came to it. "It says here that it's located at Pier Fifteen."

"Can you pull that up on a map?"

She began hacking away at the keyboard again. Up popped a map, with a red marker just on the eastern edge of Manhattan. "Right there," she said.

"Interesting," Eliza said. "Can you drop some more markers in?"

"Sure, what do you want?"

Eliza leaned in. "The three places we were fighting today."

Hai Ling shrugged her shoulders and plugged the three street corners into the map.

"Wow," said David as he studied the screen.

Rupert covered his mouth. "Oh my goodness."

The three locations formed a sort of semicircle, all around the exact location of the yacht.

"In each one of the attacks, we were pushed backward," said Frederick, pointing to the screen. "Away from the yacht."

Hai Ling chewed on a pencil. "Maybe it's just a coincidence," she said. "I mean, what do these things have to do with each other?"

"But why would they take Jeremiah to the yacht?" Rupert asked. "I don't get it."

"Put yourself in the head of a fallen angel," responded Frederick. "If you had the chance to lure one of us away, wouldn't you? One of us would make a pretty great prize to show Abaddon."

They continued to argue back and forth about it, but Eliza was already holding the phone. "I think Frederick's right," she said as she punched in the number for Officer Kelly of the NYPD. "I bet that security guard is either under control of a fallen angel or is a fallen angel himself."

"But how can you be so sure?" protested Rupert. She held her hand up toward him and the phone to her ear.

"Hi, Officer Kelly, this is Eliza Stone," she said. "I know you're busy, but I have some information that we think might help us. I think I saw one of the men."

She paused.

"No, on television. He was standing behind the Russian ambassador."

"Yes, I know that sounds a little crazy, but I think somehow they might be connected. He has this boat . . ."

"Yes, I know it's been all over the news. His yacht, well, we think that maybe . . . it's where Jeremiah is."

Eliza closed her eyes and started to pace around the room as the others watched.

"I know, I know, you are busy and are working hard to find him. I'm just trying to help . . ."

"Yes, yes," she said, her voice growing quiet. "You'll check it out, then? Okay . . . bye."

She sat down in one of the soft chairs. "Officer Kelly said they'd check it out," she said. "But she kind of blew me off."

"Why didn't you tell her about the attacks?" Carlo said.

"What was I supposed to do, tell her we were beaten back by fallen angels?"

Eliza stood again. "There's something there. I really think that's the same man who took Jeremiah. And why would we all be pushed back by a huge force of fallen angels, away from the direction of the boat?"

"There are probably a lot of reasonable explanations here," suggested Rupert, always eager to avoid a fight. "If we can just think for a few minutes . . ."

"You guys can think," answered Eliza, moving toward the steps. "I'm going to check it out. Anyone who wants to come with me, well, come on."

She didn't wait for anyone to decide. She simply headed up the steps. But it didn't take long for her to hear footsteps.

Waiting in the hallway, Eliza watched as they all emerged through the doorway, surrounding her.

"We're with you, Eliza," Julia said. The others nodded. "Lead the way."

Eliza barked out instructions as they hurried down the city streets, back toward the place where they'd been turned away earlier by Abaddon's forces.

"We need to find a way to get past the Fallen," she said. They all agreed that if they were watching the streets, they'd be guarding subway stations too.

A city bus drove by, spitting exhaust fumes in their direction. Frederick snapped his fingers. "I have an idea."

They were still in the hidden realm, and the bus that had stopped at the street corner to pick up passengers was filled. Frederick was studying the bus map plastered against the bus stop wall.

"That's the one we want. Follow me! Quickly!" he said, and began to run toward the back of the bus. He jumped onto the back bumper and, using the door handle like the rung of a ladder, pushed himself upward, and with the grace of a gymnast, he was on top of the bus in seconds.

He stuck his hand down and helped pull up David, who in turn began pulling up the rest of the quarterlings along with Frederick. They were all easy, except for Andre. His foot had barely lifted off the ground when the bus began to move. Both David and Frederick had to yank him as hard as they could, Frederick turning red in the face as he strained and wrestled the big Russian to the top of the bus.

"Don't you think the fallen angels can see us up here?" Hai Ling said as they sat on top of the moving vehicle. Rupert was nodding his agreement.

"No, this is a good idea," Eliza said. "They might see us if they think to look up here, but we'll be moving faster than we normally would, and who knows, we just might get lucky."

"Well, it's a good thing the top of this bus is flat," Ruth said.

"Thank you, Ruth," Frederick said. "I can always count on you to see the positives. Unlike some of the rest of you here."

He glanced toward Hai Ling and Rupert, who were scowling but said nothing.

Eliza was tracking their movement on the map on her phone. The bus made three more stops, and with each one, drew closer to the boat.

"Be on the lookout!" she cautioned the others as they approached the points where they were attacked before. "Be careful! Just stay ready for anything!"

"Okay, okay, Eliza," said Frederick. "Take a deep breath or something."

"It looks like we're only a couple of blocks from the yacht's location," said Rupert, studying his own phone.

Most of the quarterlings were watching the sky, but so far, they'd seen nothing.

"Maybe we're going to get lucky after all," Eliza whispered.

Ruth, who was the only one looking down, pointed at the street ahead. "Look!" she said, a smile on her face. "It's a cute little puppy, walking all by himself."

The girls moved toward the front of the bus to see. A scruffy dog was standing on the street corner. Gray, black, and brown, though it was unclear what was his actual color and what was dirt. It obviously hadn't been brushed or taken care of in quite some time, if ever. It seemed to be watching the bus.

"Aww," Bridget said, "he's so cute! I wonder if he's lost."

"It seems like he's looking right at us," said Ruth. "Which I know is impossible, since we're in the hidden realm. But still . . ."

The dog watched the top of the bus and then barked a couple of times. Then he walked back around the corner.

"Where's he going?" Bridget said. "You know, I was thinking just the other day that we need a pet for the convent . . ."

Several of the kids began to talk excitedly about the possibility, and they momentarily turned their eyes away from the road and the sky.

They didn't see the dog reemerge from around the corner until he was standing in front of the bus.

And he wasn't alone this time.

"Guys, I think you better take a look at this," Andre said, standing up on the bus rooftop.

Behind the dog were seven others, who looked almost identical to the small one. They started barking loudly, snarling at them. And then, they began to change. Their tails grew long and pointed. Claws grew out of their feet, a particularly sharp one coming from their front paws. Their fur was replaced by scaly, greenish skin. Their snouts extended, with mouths suddenly full of sharp teeth.

"What are those?" Rupert cried out, backing up a couple of steps.

"I don't know," said Frederick, "but it seems as if they can actually see us. Don't you think, Eliza?"

She had already pulled out her angelblade. "Yes, I'm afraid it does."

No one else could, apparently. A continuous stream of people were walking down the street, but no one looked over at the creatures.

"They look like some kind of giant lizard," said David, pulling an arrow off his back and stringing it to the bow, which had appeared in his left hand. "But not like anything I've ever seen."

The creatures leaped forward, over the cars that were in front of them, like they were small fences, easily cleared. Eliza swallowed hard as she moved to the front of the bus.

As the bus moved forward, the lizards ran beside it, jumping up and slamming their heads into the side of it.

"Move to the middle, everyone!" Eliza called out. They crowded toward the center of the roof, but just then the bus turned to the right. Hai Ling lost her balance and fell backward, her body dropping off the side. Only her two hands were visible, having grabbed onto the low-hanging rack that went around the top.

"Ahhhhh!" she screamed. "Help! Help!"

The creatures all moved to her side, eager for a feast. Wide-eyed, she kicked downward as hard as she could, meeting one of the animals in the nose.

"David, Lania. Arrows!" Frederick called out as he reached down for her hands. David aimed down and released an arrow. Lania strung one of her own and did the same. Each of them hit a giant lizard squarely. It tumbled to the ground, rolling along the asphalt road behind the moving bus.

Frederick had both of Hai Ling's hands in his and fell backward toward the middle. Hai Ling sprang up over the edge, landing beside him. She was still screaming, and for a second, Eliza thought she'd been bitten.

"I'm okay, I'm okay," she finally said, catching her breath.

Frederick pulled her up. "Good, because we need your arrows."

Eliza stood on the edge, swinging at any of the animals that dared jump high enough. David, Lania, Frederick, and Hai Ling stood on the edges too, firing as many arrows as they could. But it seemed like every time one of them connected with a lizard, two more emerged from the streets.

They were so busy with the creatures below they almost didn't see what was descending on them from above.

Creatures with the heads and wings of eagles and the bodies of lions swooped down from over the tops of buildings and around corners in the air. Eliza only looked up when she heard the awful screeching in the air.

"We have more trouble, guys!" she said, pointing her sword up. "Shields, quickly!"

Rupert, Julia, Carlo, and Bridget immediately shot their hands in the air, forming one large bubble, encompassing all the quarterlings still in the middle of the roof.

"What are those things?" Julia yelled, just as three of them slammed their claws into the shield. It held steady, but they could feel the impact and braced themselves against the roof. Four more dove down, with their awful sound, and slammed their heads into the shields. Carlo and Rupert both fell to one knee but bravely kept their hands up.

"I hope this bus keeps moving!" Andre shouted, gathered in the middle with the others. "If it stops, I think this could get even worse!"

Eliza snuck a glance ahead, hoping more than anything to see a tunnel. Instead, the light ahead of them turned red.

"Don't look now . . . ," said Rupert in an already defeated tone.

The bus was slowing to a stop. As it did, one of the giant lizards stood still, while another climbed on its back. They did it so fast that no one had time to react. A third animal hopped up on those two, snagged Lania by the arm with its sharp teeth, and dragged her to the street.

"Lania!" Andre shouted, running to the side. Two of the beasts were on top of her. Eliza saw only one arm and one leg from her perch above.

Without considering herself at all, Eliza hopped down,

slamming her foot into the head of the creature, and landed on the ground.

Her sword was still in her hand, and she sprung up.

"Hey!"

Swinging her blade with all her might, she sliced into one of the giant lizards on top of her friend. He immediately turned into a silver liquid, draining into the street. The other was on top of Lania, pinning her down and going for her neck. She was fighting him off with all her strength, but clearly losing.

Eliza thrust her sword forward. The lizard yelped, just before it turned into the same silvery liquid.

The bus had begun to pull forward again, though, and Eliza and Lania watched the creatures raining down from the sky, blasting themselves into the glowing but ever-weakening shield, while the gang of creatures continued its pursuit.

"They're leaving!" Lania said, leaping up. But quickly, they realized they had more pressing issues to deal with.

Four lizards surrounded them and were closing in slowly. Each had a forearm outstretched, with a long, razor-like talon held up high, ready to strike. They were small, but fierce and aggressive. And, without needing to look up, Eliza could feel the presence of creatures in the air above.

Lania had an arrow drawn, and Eliza held her sword aloft. But what could they do against all of the creatures at once?

"We have to fight, Lania," Eliza said, trying to find strength for her voice, but hearing herself shake. "No matter what, we need to fight."

The scaly lizards crept in, their fangs dripping with the prospect of a kill. They looked hungry, ready for a quarterling feast.

One of them reared its head back and let forth a terrifying screech that chilled Eliza down to her bones.

"Please, Elohim," she whispered, closing her eyes. All she could think about, the only face she could see, was Jeremiah's. She needed to be there for him, no matter what. But it didn't appear now that she would have that chance. "Please . . ."

A screeching sound, a blast of light, and the feel of something cool and wet hitting her cheek caused her eyes to pop open.

The awful lizards were gone. She and Lania were covered with silvery liquid.

Another flash above her, and the flying creatures scattered up above the buildings and out of sight.

Looking up, a figure stood above them, silhouetted by the sun behind. He held a glittering silver blade in his right hand.

Eliza blinked for a few seconds, unable to believe her eyes. "Jonah?"

TWENTY

A LITTLE PIECE OF PAPER

The fallen angel surveyed the landscape from the top corner of the building. The sun was halfway down, sending a glint of orange light across the city, but growing darker with each passing minute.

He sat curled into a ball on the edge of the rooftop wall, his blackened hands pushing against brick, holding him steady. His orders were simple, and his eyes were trained on the street below, watching and waiting.

The black car turned onto the street, moving slowly. It caught the fallen angel's attention. He watched, unmoving, as the car pulled in front of the building he was perched on, then stopped.

The driver got out and opened the back door, and the large Russian emerged.

He'd been told to wait for the ambassador here, that he always stopped at the small, exclusive bar located in the bottom of the building for a quiet drink. It was time.

The fallen angel sprang from the building, pushing himself

into the air and going into a fast dive. Just as he was almost on top of the car, he spread his wings, pulling up and landing softly behind the man. Then he jumped onto the ambassador's shoulders and began to work.

The fallen angel plowed his hands down into the man's back. The man, of course, didn't feel a thing, unaware of what was happening in the hidden realm. If he'd been a follower of Elohim, perhaps he would have recognized the threat. He would have felt the danger and asked for protection.

But the fallen angel was soon finding out, to his delight, that the man was exceedingly open to his proddings.

Other fallen angels had certainly visited this man in the past, that much was clear as he reached inside. There was so much fear and pride and darkness. It made the fallen angel almost explode with excitement.

The fallen angel looked up to see Abaddon stride around the corner. His head was covered by a dark hood, allowing only a small glimpse of his lone red eye. An army of fallen angels marched silently behind him. He glanced at the fallen angel sitting on the man's back and nodded his approval.

"Vitaly," the man said, emerging from the shadows, arms outstretched. "We meet again. Twice in one day. What are the odds?"

Vitaly looked back, surprised. "Mr. Prince," he said. Unlike the fallen angel, he saw Abaddon as a man in a dark suit by himself on the street corner. He glanced toward the building. "I'm starting to think you know my schedule better than I do."

Mr. Prince shrugged, a sly smile creeping on his lips. "Let's just say I have ways of figuring things out. I have some good people working for me." He glanced over his shoulder, back into the empty darkness, and winked.

In the hidden realm, the fallen angels behind him cackled with laughter.

The delight of the vision he'd seen in this man's eyes stirred Vitaly. How had he been able to see such things? He didn't understand it, but he desperately wanted the things he'd seen to come true. He despised this man, yet he longed to see what he had seen before. And he remembered the words from this morning.

He reached inside his jacket pocket and pulled out a folded piece of paper. "I believe this is what you requested," he said, extending it in his hand to Mr. Prince. "I hope this will satisfy whatever it is that you are looking for." His breathing became quick and choppy as he moved toward the man to hand him the paper. He shook it at him. "I don't know what you want with these names . . ."

Vitaly didn't finish his sentence, and Mr. Prince simply stood there, hands in his pockets, a strange grin on his face, watching.

"Yes?" he finally said to the Russian ambassador. "You were saying?"

Vitaly felt a fire rattling up from deep within. Something inside wanted to confront him. But he wanted to see again. The glorious image he had seen last night. He felt so confused. In the hidden realm, the fallen angel twisted and squeezed violently, enjoying the foothold he'd been given.

Vitaly took a couple of deep breaths and tried to gather himself. *Get control, Vitaly.*

He felt the piercing eyes of Mr. Prince and met them with his own.

"You want to see it again, don't you, Vitaly? What I showed you last night?"

Vitaly swallowed, trying to look away. He couldn't. His head nodded yes.

How long Vitaly stood there, whether it was a few seconds—or an hour—he didn't know. But as he remained under Mr. Prince's gaze, he felt everything inside him come to a halt. There was only one thing he wanted—power beyond imagination. It flooded his mind and body, tingling him with electricity. He was overcome with the thought of it, and his mind began to spin.

"Have you seen enough?" Mr. Prince said, already knowing the answer.

Vitaly shook his head. He wanted more.

But just like that, once again Mr. Prince blinked, and the image went dark again, like running water turned off at a sink.

"You will have more," Mr. Prince said. "You simply must continue to do what I say. It's easy, really. You help me, and I'll help you."

Vitaly's heart was suddenly a cave of darkness and despair. He craved what he'd seen, even more than last night. He nodded. "Yes."

"Hand me the paper, Vitaly," Mr. Prince said, his voice silky smooth. Vitaly's hand shot out to him. He couldn't get it into Mr. Prince's hands fast enough. Mr. Prince reached his hand out to grab it, and for a moment, neither one of them let go.

Mr. Prince's eyes flashed, and for a moment, Vitaly thought, *Could it be? Were they really red?* His mouth dropped open, and the intoxicating possibility of power vanished into emptiness. Mr. Prince blinked, and his eyes changed back to cool black.

Vitaly let go of the paper, and as he did, he gasped. It felt like a part of him left too, some piece of him on the inside that had been cut loose from the rest, choosing now to exit. Given to this man along with the folded paper.

Somehow, Vitaly knew that Mr. Prince felt this too, that this transfer was more than just names on a list.

"That was easy, wasn't it?"

Vitaly drew his eyes away, down to his own shoes. "This is a list you could have gotten a variety of ways," he said. "Why did you need it from me?"

Mr. Prince cocked his head to the side. "Look up at me again, Vitaly."

Vitaly's eyes popped up quickly.

"Yes, perhaps I could have gotten this somewhere else. In fact . . ." He held it up, and then began to tear it into pieces. In an instant, there were a hundred tiny scraps in his hand, and he let them fall to the ground.

Vitaly felt his anger rise. "Why did you do that? Why make me go to this kind of trouble for you?"

Mr. Prince smiled, stuffing his hands in his pockets again. "I didn't really care about the list, Vitaly. I already know who's coming to your party, and yes, I will be there too, by the way. I have something special planned for this party, you see."

Vitaly stood, bewildered, as Mr. Prince turned and began to walk away. He spun back around, though, his eyes gleaming. Red again. "Just one more thing. You did that for me. Is that clear? You did it for me. Did you feel that? When we held the paper there together?"

Vitaly swallowed hard, not believing this man could know how he'd felt in that moment. How did he know what was going on deep inside of him? "You . . . you . . . ?" He couldn't even put a sentence together.

"Yes, Vitaly," he said. "I have a part of you now. Soon, I'll have all of you. I own you. Isn't that cool? You'll get what you want too, remember?" Mr. Prince held his arms out wide, looking up to the heavens. "I own a piece of this guy's soul! How about that?" It was as if he were shouting it not at Vitaly as much as to an unknown face in the sky. He stepped back closer to Vitaly again, leaning right into his face.

"And when the time comes," he whispered, "you'll again do exactly as I say. You've already proven you would, by getting me this worthless sheet of names. And now, I have you in my back pocket. I can't wait to have the rest of your friends there too."

Vitaly crumpled against the trunk of his car. "My . . . my power?"

Mr. Prince seemed to barely hear him as he walked away. He waved a dismissive hand in the air. "Yes, yes, you'll have what you crave. In a manner of speaking."

Vitaly's heart leaped and sank, all at once, knowing that his relationship with Mr. Prince was nowhere near over.

TWENTY-ONE

NO TIME FOR REUNIONS

Jonah reached his hand down to his sister. She stared at him for a few seconds, started to scowl, but then let him help her to her feet. He knew she had so many questions, and he wanted to answer them all.

But right now, they were still under attack. And so were their friends.

"I know, Eliza, there's a lot you want to know, and a lot I want to say," he said. He wiped a swath of the silvery liquid off her arm and onto his finger. "Gross. I had no idea those lizards would turn into gray goo."

Lania hugged him tightly. "Jonah! I can't believe it's really you!"

He blushed. "Hey, at least somebody's glad I'm back."

Eliza frowned at him. "I can't believe you . . ."

"Let's go help the others first, okay?" he said. Grabbing Eliza's and Lania's hands, he began to run after the bus.

"Hang on tight!" he said as his feet became a blur. He lifted them up in each arm, and they sped down the road in search of the bus.

It wasn't hard to find, since it was the only one under attack.

"Griffins!" he exclaimed as he saw the half-bird, half-lions. "I should have guessed."

He came up behind the vehicle and slowed down just enough to drop Eliza and Lania at the back.

"Eliza, see if you can take care of the rest of these lizards, just like I did back there," he said, looking upward to the sky. "I need to do something about these bird brains."

"I've got it covered," she said. Jonah was struck by the new confidence he heard in her voice.

They both pulled out their angelblades at the same time, Eliza moving around the bus and Jonah climbing up the back. Within seconds, he'd pulled himself up.

"Need some help?" he asked, but everyone was too busy to even notice he was there.

The creatures were swooping down one after another and were very adept at dodging arrows. They were descending, claws first and outstretched, and Jonah knew exactly what they were trying to do. He'd seen it before.

The griffins wanted a piece of their hearts.

Jonah had no idea if they could actually reach inside a quarterling and latch onto that deepest part of him with Elohim's protection. But he sure didn't want to find out.

He raised his sword in the air and stood beside the others, who finally noticed he was there.

"Jonah! It's about time!" Andre shouted, fending off one of them.

"Where have *you* been?" demanded an exasperated Rupert from behind his shield.

Frederick called out to him from across the top of the bus while he shot a flaming arrow. "Nice of you to join us!"

"Yeah, yeah!" Jonah shouted. "Save it for later!"

The bus turned to the left, and Ruth fell backward, her head dangling over the side of the bus. Jonah quickly reached down and grabbed her foot, yanking her back to the middle.

But he'd taken his eyes off the griffins, and they were fast, faster than he anticipated. He felt claws tearing into him before he could turn around.

"Aaaahhh!" He felt searing pain in his shoulder and something digging around inside him. The weight of the creature pushed him flat on his stomach. The griffin's claws were reaching, searching, and trying to pry something loose.

As it did, suddenly his vision grew blurry. He was no longer on top of the bus. He was in the backyard, throwing the football with his father on a sunny, warm day beside the pond. Then he was kneeling in church at the altar, with his mother and father standing behind him. The church was filled with the soaring voices of the choir. He was in the neighborhood pool, being baptized by his dad, watching his mother's face fill with tears of joy.

Then those scenes all began to fade at once. They were being pulled, prodded, and tugged until he felt as if they were going to be somehow yanked out of his heart, like batteries from a remote control. He was losing them. They were disappearing, fading away from him like they were falling slowly into a deep hole. He felt hazy.

I have to get up. I have to get up . . .

Jonah kept telling himself to move, but all of his limbs were suddenly made of lead. He barely had enough strength to turn his head to the side and open his eyes.

He saw a foggy scene in front of him. All the quarterlings

who had been fighting on the rooftop of the bus were down, lying either on their backs or stomachs. Each one of them had one of the griffins digging inside of him or her.

A flash of green light caught his eye. The bus had stopped at another light, and Eliza had climbed back up onto the roof. Her blade was in her hand.

Jonah's eyes opened a little wider, and he tried to will his hand to move. But he couldn't do it.

"Elohim . . . ," he whispered. "Help."

His hand suddenly felt a little lighter . . .

Jonah reached toward his side and made a pulling motion with his hand. He felt the angelblade appear. The blade was in his hand, the tip right in front of his face, casting a soft glow. The griffin had his arm pinned down with one of its claws, though, and he could barely move it.

He strained against the monster on his back, trying to summon all his strength, focusing it into his right hand. Pushing as hard as he could against the roof, he was able to move it just a little. One inch, two inches, just a little more . . .

Jonah flicked his wrist backward, slicing into the claw of the creature. Its awful scream filled his ears, but its grip loosened. He turned around as fast as he could and ripped his blade across the chest of the griffin. Its scream faded, and it fell into a pile of feathers and fur beside him.

He stood up, wobbly, gathering himself, and turned to the closest quarterling, David.

Jonah moved as fast as he could, swiping at the creature on top of David with his sword. Eliza worked from the other side of the bus. He just hoped they weren't too late.

They met the last griffin in the middle together, and both of their swords tore through it at the same time. It fell off Rupert, who looked dazed.

Slowly, Rupert pushed himself up on his elbows. "I was . . . it felt like I was dreaming about something . . ." He rubbed his bleary eyes. "Thank you."

But then he looked past them with horror, and words had stopped coming from his mouth.

Whipping around just in time, Jonah met one last griffin. He drove his blade through its chest, and they watched it flop lifelessly to the ground.

"Everyone all right?" Eliza called out. They all nodded their heads.

The bus was still picking up passengers underneath them.

"Let's get out of here," Frederick said, hitting himself on the side of the head, trying to shake the grogginess out. They hopped down from the bus just before it pulled off.

They were still in the hidden realm as they gathered together on the street, invisible to passersby. The quarterlings surrounded Jonah.

"You're back!" Julia said with a huge smile, hugging him tightly around the neck. "We were all worried sick about you."

"So good to see you again, finally, my friend!" David said, hugging Jonah too. "It wasn't the same around here without you."

"I think even I missed you," said Frederick with a wry grin. They all chuckled.

"It's good to be back, everyone," Jonah said. "I can't wait to tell you what's been going on. But there's no time now."

He noticed one person hanging back from the rest. He stepped away from the others and walked toward her.

"Eliza, I want to explain . . ."

She crossed her arms and turned away from him.

"I know you're upset . . . I can only imagine what you've been going through here . . ."

"You can only imagine? Only imagine?" she shot back. "I've been worried sick! I've been taking care of Jeremiah. I've been trying to hold myself together . . . I've been trying to fill your shoes around here. I don't think you could even imagine what that's like!"

Jonah kept his clear, blue eyes trained on her. "I know, Eliza. It's just that, when Mom died, I needed to get away. You know that. I wanted to run. I tried . . . believe me," he said, thinking about his adventure on the bus.

"You're not the only one who lost a mother!" she said, hot tears spilling down her cheeks.

It hit him like a basketball to the nose. Of course he knew it, but he had been so wrapped up in himself that he'd forgotten—Eliza and Jeremiah were going through the same things he was. They had just chosen to deal with it differently.

All of his defensiveness and desire to explain himself melted away. It could wait. "I know," he said softly. He felt tears of his own fall, and he didn't stop them. "I'm sorry."

Instead of pulling herself away, she leaned toward him. He pulled her shoulders to him and held her close. They were quiet for a few seconds, and then both of them pushed back and quickly wiped the tears off their faces.

The rest of the quarterlings were watching their reunion, and Frederick began a slow clap.

Eliza snorted into her shirtsleeve and glared at them. "What are you all looking at?"

TWENTY-TWO

THE BIG BOAT

H ow did you find us, anyway?" Eliza said, having cooled a little.

"You're welcome for saving your rear end, by the way," answered Jonah. He couldn't help getting in a little dig to his sister, even under these circumstances. "I got to the convent just after you left. The rooftop angels have a pretty good sense of what's going on. It wasn't hard to get them to point me in the right direction. And once I was in the hidden realm, it was easy to see where you guys were fighting."

Several of the quarterlings sitting down were holding their heads in their hands. The confrontation with the beasts had shaken them up. Jonah was still feeling a little groggy himself.

"That was a weird feeling, wasn't it?" David said to Jonah as he leaned over to comfort Carlo. "It wasn't just like someone was reaching down into my chest. It was like they were digging around in my soul or something."

Jonah nodded. "I saw these creatures at work back in Peacefield, when I was home." He felt awkward as he said it, knowing he'd been there only because he left them behind. "An angel there showed me what they were doing. Trying to tug at hearts and souls, all under the direction of Abaddon, of course. It was an awful thing to watch. They are dangerous creatures. If they'd gotten to us, it would all be over."

"Those bird-like creatures, as well as the lizards . . . I remember some places in the Old Testament that refer to both. Isaiah and Leviticus come to mind," David said. He turned to watch the quarterlings sitting in front of him. "But what concerns me now is that I'm not sure all of us can make it to the yacht."

Jonah knelt down in front of them, placing a hand on Lania's shoulder. "Why don't you take everyone injured back, David?"

David blinked at him. "I want to help find your brother, Jonah," he said. But he looked back down at the quarterlings again. He sighed. "But maybe you're right. Our friends here look like they could use the attention of the nuns."

Eliza nodded. "I agree. Take them back and protect them on the way. The rest of us can handle this, can't we, Jonah?"

He nodded, slapping his sister on the back. "That's right. Now, time to go."

"Bless them, Elohim," David called out, eyes pointing upward in spontaneous prayer. "Be with them, guard their path, direct their steps, and ensure their victory. And mine as well."

After they said their good-byes, Jonah, Eliza, Frederick, Andre, Julia, and Hai Ling moved down a dark alleyway together.

"I'm glad you are coming, Hai Ling," Jonah said, unable to hide his surprise at her decision to forge ahead.

She shrugged and scratched the corner of her eye. "Whatever.

I've kind of . . . grown attached to your little brother." She glanced away, and Jonah wondered if it was so he wouldn't see her tears.

Quickly, Eliza filled him in on the information they had gathered, repeating the story she had told for what felt like a hundred times to the police about Jeremiah's capture, and then the Russian ambassador and the man she saw on television.

"I know it seems like a hunch," she admitted, "but it was more than that. I felt like Elohim, somehow, was showing me that he was the same guy I saw take Jeremiah."

"Sounds like it's all we have to go on anyway," said Jonah. "And if you think Elohim was leading you, how am I going to argue with that? So, lead the way, E."

She eyed him cautiously, and he realized it would probably take some time before she would accept that he was back. He hoped they'd have time to really talk later. But for now, the plan was simple—find Jeremiah and get him back, unharmed.

"Do you think he's really seeing her?" Jonah asked as they walked. "Seeing Mom?"

"Jonah, how is that possible? We both saw her die, didn't we?"

He nodded. "Yeah. We did. It's hard to get too mad at him about this, though. Maybe it's his way of, you know, missing her."

"Well, maybe someone's tricking him," she said, darkness in her eyes.

Jonah pressed his lips together. He'd already thought of that. "Let's don't assume the worst."

"Be very careful, everyone," Eliza said, keeping her eyes trained on the rooftops above. "We need to move as fast as we can and get to that yacht before anyone—or anything—else sees us."

The wind was picking up, and the sun had completely set. It was cold, a blustery frozen winter night that sent chills up and down Jonah's back. "Wish I'd remembered my coat," he muttered, rubbing his bare arms with his hands. He was still wearing the T-shirt he had changed into after the game. After the bus accident, he had caught another bus, directly to New York, poring over Eliza's text all the way there, hoping and praying he would arrive in time to help find their brother.

Jonah hadn't called Eliza on the way, deciding that he'd rather talk to her in person first. But he had decided to call his dad, about an hour before the bus was set to arrive. They really talked for what felt like the first time all year. Jonah told his dad everything. He knew it was a lot for his father to take at once, but he had to know. Jonah figured his dad would be in New York soon.

"It should be two more blocks this way," said Frederick, studying the map on his phone. "We're almost at the waterfront." He glanced over at Jonah walking beside him. "You left so fast last year. I never really got to say it . . . but I'm sorry about your mom. I truly am."

Jonah nodded at Frederick, and he was surprised that he could barely remember what the South African boy had been like two years before when they'd met. He'd been so arrogant, but he'd changed a lot since then. The old Frederick was still in there, somewhere, and occasionally got out, but change was happening. Elohim was really working in Frederick's life.

"Thanks," Jonah answered. "It's been a hard year for everybody."

"We're not going to let the same thing happen to your brother," he added.

The words hung in the air as they crept down the barely lit street. Jonah had tried to push the thought out of his mind—the one that reminded him that there was a very good chance that they wouldn't find Jeremiah.

"I think the water is just ahead," Jonah said. They could make out a bridge lit up, and they could see the red brake lights of cars moving slowly across the East River. Wind whipped off the water, funneling down their block, and Jonah grimaced as it hit his face.

Eliza stopped before they rounded the corner. "The yacht is supposed to be docked just down this street," she said, pointing behind her. "We're in the hidden realm, so we ought to be able to sneak on board without too much trouble. That will be the easy part."

Frederick chuckled. "Yeah, we know. The hard part is not getting seen by any of the nonhuman bad guys."

But she was hopeful. "When we find him, we ought to be able to just walk right off with him. No one will know."

"How do you think they're holding him, though?" Hai Ling asked, a frown on her face. "Shouldn't he just be able to walk away anyway? I mean, just enter the hidden realm and escape."

"Yes, I was actually kind of wondering the same thing," said Julia.

Eliza tugged at her lip. "I don't know, and I have to admit, I've had those thoughts too. But the last I checked, none of us can walk out of an unlocked door, can we? We can't walk through walls. It's possible he's stuck somewhere. Anyway, it's time to go see. Just be on your guard."

They stepped around the corner, and ahead, docked on a long pier, was an enormous ship. It was mostly black and spanned almost the entire length of the pier. Blue lights ran the length of it, giving off a strange glow.

"That's a big boat," said Frederick, whistling. "I've seen some large ones in South Africa before. But nothing close to that."

"It looks bigger than a football field," Jonah said. He turned to Eliza. "That's going to be a lot of rooms to search."

She walked faster, buoyed by the actual sight of the ambassador's vessel. "The faster we get there, the quicker we can find him and get out of here."

I sure hope she's right, Jonah said. He wanted to grab Jeremiah, maybe give him a shake or two for running off on his own, and then speed back to the safety of the convent as quickly as possible.

He studied the boat as they approached. There was a long ramp that connected the yacht to the dock, and people in fancy clothes were all walking up onto the boat that way.

"There are people getting on," Andre observed. "Looks like a lot of them."

"And there are a lot of black limousines parked out in front," Jonah said, pointing down the street. Several were pulling up, and a few had dropped off their passengers and were leaving. "They're all dressed up. It looks like we're not going to be the only ones on this ship tonight."

As they drew closer, and the boat became more visible with its upper deck lit up with music blaring, Jonah only felt a deeper darkness. The cold wind whipped, but the chill he felt had nothing to do with that. Something swept over him that almost made him stop.

"Did you guys feel that?" he asked tentatively.

"Yes," said Julia, shivering beside him and stopping in the middle of the street. "I feel . . . a sadness. It's hard to describe. There is something very, very bad on that boat."

"Yeah, I did too," said Andre.

Jonah looked at the yacht, and then back at Julia. "There's an evil there. I can feel it." He took a few steps to stand beside her. But what were they going to do, just leave? They couldn't abandon the search—not if there was a chance Jeremiah was on that boat. "We have to do this, Julia. For Jeremiah, remember? Elohim is with us. Even in the darkness."

She shivered again, studying the lights on the coastline across the water for a few seconds. Finally, she nodded, turning into the wind again.

"It won't take us long," said Eliza, "and then we'll be off this boat and back home again."

Jonah stepped ahead, trying to at least appear brave in front of the rest. But he was shuddering inside, as much as any of the others. It was a coldness, and one he'd felt before.

They scanned the top of the boat and all along the streets for signs of fallen angels, but, so far, they'd seen none. As they approached, though, Frederick pointed high.

"Up there, at the top!" he whispered. "Four fallen angels, on guard!" He pulled them down behind a garbage bin.

Jonah watched the fallen ones pace back and forth up above. They were watching the people board the boat. There was a security check at the front of the ramp where two officers were using scanners and checking purses.

"There must be some famous people here," said Andre. "They look fancy, and they're all getting scanned."

They watched for another minute before Eliza spoke. "We have to get on this boat," she muttered. "There seems to be only one way on. Here's what we're going to have to do . . ."

After they'd huddled for a minute more, with Jonah keeping a careful eye above, they waited until he gave the signal. He watched the guards pacing slowly, trying to find a moment when they were all turned away.

"Okay, go!" he said, and the six of them scurried out and into the street. The line of people boarding was right there, and they each quickly found a place in between a couple, spreading themselves out in the line and just trying to mix in with the crowd.

"Keep your heads down. Whatever you do, don't look up, and you should blend right in!" Eliza had told them.

Jonah was almost at the end, sandwiched behind a couple who were both very short and very wide, and in front of another couple who both had the tanned faces and chiseled features of supermodels.

Why did I decide to get behind the short people? He kicked himself for finding this spot, but he didn't want to risk changing and giving the fallen angels above another reason to look.

I guess if they saw us, we'll be hearing from them soon.

But as the line progressed forward, he realized they apparently hadn't been seen yet. Andre appeared to be having the toughest time of it as the largest of the quarterlings. He peered back at Jonah a couple of times, looking as if he were trying to hold his breath, as he had wedged himself closely between two very talkative couples.

If he ended up touching them . . .

Jonah quietly prayed that they would all be able to make it through the line without shocking any of the guests with an accidental touch.

He shuffled along, trying to keep his eyes on the wooden pier beneath his feet.

"What an opportunity," the supermodel woman behind him murmured. "I can't believe we're getting to do this, James. Everyone who is anyone in politics is going to be on this little boat." She trilled with laughter at her joke.

Jonah heard James, the other supermodel, lean in. "You-know-who is in town, dear. You never know. Rumor is, he might be making an appearance as well."

This caused her giddy laugh to rise even louder, and Jonah wondered whom it was they were referring to. But the way they were speaking, he thought he had a good guess.

The short, portly woman in front of him turned and looked directly at him. He panicked for a second before reminding himself that there was no way she could see him. She wore an enormous strand of jewels around her neck, and he was close enough to see the caked-on makeup over her eyes and along her cheeks.

"Darling," she drooled, "have you never met the POTUS before? What a pity."

Jonah was all of a sudden stuck in the middle of a conversation.

"POTUS?" The supermodel was clearly confused.

The short man turned around, smiling at her, and eyeing her up and down. He took her hand in his, reaching right around Jonah, so that he had to stretch himself like a pretzel to avoid getting touched. "You know, the president of the United States. POTUS. He's a personal friend of ours. I'd be happy to introduce you if he does indeed arrive." He nodded to James. "And your friend, of course."

Jonah was having a hard time keeping his eyes on all four people surrounding him, to make sure no one reached out and put their hand through him or leaned in a little too close.

Apparently, though, someone up ahead hadn't been so lucky because a woman screamed.

Jonah looked ahead, like everyone else in the line, trying to figure out what was going on. Andre stepped out of the line, his face bright red. The woman standing behind him was shaking her head and holding her chest.

"Something shocked me!" she was saying. "Who did that?"

TWENTY-THREE

HEARING THINGS

But no one around her had any answers. A man, who identified himself as a doctor, came over and checked her out, but she appeared unharmed.

"Andre!" Jonah whispered, peeking up to see the fallen angels above, staring down at them. Andre was still standing outside the line, watching the woman and scratching his head. "Andre!"

He turned toward Jonah and raised both hands in the air. *What am I supposed to do?* he was saying.

Jonah pointed ahead. "Get back in line," he said.

Andre glanced up and then slowly moved closer to the line.

The Fallen watched for another minute, but then kept pacing around the top deck. Jonah breathed a sigh of relief.

They were moving forward, at least, and Eliza and Julia had reached the ramp. They walked across it slowly and finally made it to the end, disappearing inside the door of the yacht. Hai Ling and Frederick were next. Hai Ling looked back at Jonah several times, and he could tell she was nervous. But with Frederick's encouragement, she made it.

Jonah watched Andre go, trying to stay within the gap, and he prayed that somehow Andre wouldn't touch anyone again.

Jonah kept his head down as he walked across the ramp, sensing the darkness again, growing heavier with each step. Folding his arms across his chest, he tried not to let the shivering fear overtake him. He wondered if any of the people who were laughing and carrying on all around him felt anything at all.

"We all made it," said a relieved Eliza when Jonah met them just inside the doorway, underneath a stairwell. She glared at Andre. "Barely."

"What was I supposed to do?" he protested. "That woman just backed up into me. I couldn't move out of the way fast enough."

Jonah watched the guests file up the staircase above their heads. He figured they were heading for the top deck.

"Forget it," Frederick said. "We made it on this ship. Now what? Anyone have a clue where to go?"

Jonah was about to suggest that they split up and search the boat in pairs so that they could find Jeremiah faster.

"I'm not splitting up," said Hai Ling. "No offense to anyone here, but there's something sinister on this yacht. I can feel it, and it's creeping me out."

She shuddered visibly, and although Jonah thought the others would protest, Julia and Andre both nodded their heads.

"Okay, then," he said, looking at Eliza. "Want to all stay together?"

"Considering everything we're all feeling, that might be the best thing to do."

"Let's go floor by floor," said Julia. "It's a huge boat, but it shouldn't take too long if we move quickly."

They agreed that it would make the most sense to start at the top and move down, if they needed to, into the lower levels of the boat. Jonah led the way up the staircase, following the passengers upstairs until they were just below the top deck. A small spiral staircase led one more level up, and the last of the guests were on it.

"This is the level below the top," Jonah said. "I don't think Jeremiah's going to be up there in the open."

Frederick turned the handle of a door. It opened up into a narrow hallway. "This looks like a good place to start."

Eliza pushed herself in front of him. "You know I don't even need say it, but keep your eyes open and alert for fallen angels. If we can get out of here without being spotted . . ."

"It will be a miracle," Andre finished her sentence.

As they began to move down the hallway, a woman emerged from a door at the end, moving toward them quickly.

"Step to the side, step to the side!" Eliza said.

She was wearing black pants and a white dress shirt with a bow tie, carrying a tray of food on her shoulder. She was in a hurry.

Andre sniffed the air as she passed by. "Shrimp," he said excitedly. "I think that was shrimp!"

"Missing dinner, are we?" said Frederick, patting Andre on the stomach. Andre nodded sadly.

"Well, we're not here to eat," snapped Eliza. "But I think we've found the kitchen."

This was confirmed again when two more waiters, carrying their own trays full of delicious-smelling food, followed the other down the hallway. The quarterlings stood to the side again, Jonah having to duck not to get hit in the face by the trays, held aloft in the air.

"There are other rooms down here that we should check," Eliza said. "We need to be thorough."

Jonah tugged on a doorknob across from the kitchen entrance. It opened into a closet, full of all kinds of dry goods. "I think it's just a pantry," he said, pulling the door back shut.

They opened three other doors along the hall, two containing some type of kitchen supplies. The third appeared to be some kind of break room for the staff, with a round table, chairs, and a small television set. "Nothing here," Julia said, peering into the small, dark room.

They moved down to the other end of the hallway, back past the spiral staircase.

"Now this is quite different," said Frederick with a low whistle. A door to a room was open in front of them, and through it, they could see a fancy sofa, a couple of lamps, a flat-screen television turned on to a twenty-four-hour news station, and a bank of huge windows.

Suddenly, a man emerged, straightening his black bow tie. They slammed themselves against the wall as he strode by, Andre's head making a thunking sound. The man paused for a second, as if he had heard something. But, seeing nothing, he shook his head and hurried past them, bounding up the staircase.

"That was him," said Eliza. "That was Ambassador Cherkov."

"The guy who owns this boat?" asked Hai Ling.

Eliza nodded.

"Then this must be the master suite," Hai Ling said, and without waiting for the others, she moved into the huge room directly underneath a crystal chandelier.

"Hai Ling," Jonah said. "Wait for us, all right?"

"This is pretty fantastic, don't you think?" she gushed. "Even if there is a creepy feeling I still get on this ship. I mean, look at the view!"

Eliza stood with her hands on her hips. "We don't have time for you to do a yacht tour of the rich and famous, Hai Ling. He's obviously not here."

Eliza turned and strode out of the room, followed by the rest, with Hai Ling taking up the rear.

"I just wanted to check out the view," she muttered.

There were two more rooms on that hall, smaller, but just as nicely decorated, but both were empty.

"This hall's clear," said Jonah. "Let's go down one more and do it again."

They went down the steps again in a single-file line, having to avoid two more servers on the way.

"Must be quite a party they're having," Hai Ling said longingly, watching the servers pass.

"Focus, Hai Ling," said Julia. "I know you love all of this glamorous stuff, but we're not here for that right now."

Jonah led the way into the next floor, which was another series of rooms. These were all smaller guest rooms, as well as what appeared to be sleeping quarters for the crew. A quick search of the rooms found them to be entirely empty, with no one in the hallway.

The next level down was back where they entered the boat. Two guards stood beside the doorway where the ramp led back down to the pier. They were husky men with thick necks and earpieces on their ears. Jonah saw the glimmer of a gun inside one man's jacket, attached to his waist. They were watching the ramp closely, and in silence, even though no one was coming up anymore. He saw two more stationed at the bottom, the ones who'd been scanning the guests.

"They're taking this seriously, don't you think?" he murmured as they moved past the guards, invisible.

"I'm pretty sure I saw the prime minister of South Africa in line earlier," said Frederick. "They'd do well to guard this yacht carefully."

There were two hallways to search on this level, just like the last. This one, however, seemed dedicated to entertainment. On one end was a large game room, with a pool table, video games, and six large flat-screen televisions on the wall.

"This wouldn't be a bad place to watch a soccer match, would it?" Andre said, touching the soft leather of the club chairs in front of the TVs.

"No Jeremiah," said Eliza. "Come on, guys. Let's keep going."

They inspected a workout room, full of state-of-the-art gym equipment, a locker room with a sauna and showers, and then a small movie theater. All of them sat empty, and there was no sign of the missing quarterling.

Jonah felt the darkness hit him again as they walked back down the red-carpeted hallway, so hard that it almost made him stumble. He leaned against the wall for a second, trying to clear his head.

"You okay?" asked Julia.

Another voice spoke to him as well, though.

I know who you are. I know you're here.

Come on down.

TWENTY-FOUR

THREE LEVELS BELOW

Jonah heard the voice inside his head, a whisper but loud, filling up his skull. He blinked for a few seconds, looking at the others, knowing instantly that he wasn't the only one who'd heard it.

"Who said that?" Hai Ling asked, looking up and down the hallway. "Did you guys hear that?"

"For a second I thought it was just in my head," answered Jonah. "You heard it too?"

They nodded, all looking at him at once. As if he should have some kind of answer.

The truth was, he'd heard that voice before, in his worst nightmares and in person. Jonah knew exactly who it was—Abaddon. But there was no reason to scare his friends any more than they already were.

"That voice . . . ," Julia said, unable to finish her sentence. She was shaking. "I've never heard anything so . . ."

"Evil?" Andre suggested. "Me neither."

"Come on," Jonah said, moving into the stairwell and heading down to the next level. "We have to finish searching. The sooner we do that and get out of here, the better off we're all going to be."

The map on the wall indicated that they were on the main level, and that there were three more levels below, including the engine room at the very bottom.

"Let's go, guys," Eliza said as cheerily as she could muster. They were all hesitating, including her. "Let's push through this. It won't take long, like Jonah said."

Her words were less than inspiring, but they trudged down the steps. Red lights lined the halls on the next level, making everything seem gloomy and more sinister than before.

"I think it's some kind of safety lighting," said Frederick, staring up at the red glow from the lights on the wall. "Nice. Doesn't really help the situation, now, does it?"

Jonah felt a chill ripple through his body as they went down below the main deck. The others were shivering too, and he wondered if this level was used as some sort of cold storage. But there was still no sign of Jeremiah in any of the rooms filled with equipment and supplies. So they moved another level down.

"It's a giant swimming pool," Frederick said. They were, indeed, standing in front of an Olympic-sized, eight-lane pool. A bank of solid glass ran along the wall. "Must be nice to come take a swim down here when it gets too hot up top."

The pool was illuminated by that same soft glow of red, though, which made it seem creepy instead of relaxing. "I don't think I'd like to be swimming in a pool that looked like it was full of . . ." Eliza didn't finish her sentence, but Jonah knew what she was going to say.

Full of blood.

At one end of the pool was a door.

"Let's be thorough," Eliza said, and hurried over to open the door. "Pool supplies," she said, disappointed. "Just what I thought."

"Come on, Eliza," Jonah said, trying to encourage her. "There are still two levels left. Maybe he's down there."

"I just thought that he was here. Like, actually on this boat," she said, tears welling into her eyes. "When I saw that man behind the ambassador, it just seemed like he was the man I saw take Jeremiah. But now . . . now I don't know, maybe I was wrong. I wanted to believe that we could find him, so my mind tricked me or something. We should just leave, before we get in over our heads." She rubbed her arms, shivering.

Jonah felt the heaviness of evil like a blanket on top of them all. He suddenly wondered if she was right. Maybe they should just go. The coldness, the hardness of the place, was pushing out all of the hope inside him, spiraling like water down a drain. He leaned back against the wall, closing his eyes as he leaned over, hands on his knees.

"Elohim . . . ," he whispered the word, more a cry of desperation than of worship or anything else.

A singular picture came into his mind of the day Jeremiah learned to ride a bike. Jonah was riding along beside him on his own, shouting, laughing, urging him on. Benjamin and Eleanor were behind Jeremiah, cheering, and there to catch him if he fell. Jeremiah's face was full of untamed joy, his mouth hanging open, his hair blowing back, his eyes wide.

"Whhhheeeeeeeeeeeeee!" he shouted. Jonah laughed and cheered.

The image came and left his mind in an instant. But it was enough.

"Let's finish this," Jonah said, pushing back off the wall. He grabbed Eliza's hand and took it in his. "If Jeremiah's here, we'll know soon."

He moved and beckoned the others to follow. Steeling himself, he led them down another level.

The steps let out into yet another hallway, and Jonah stuck his head out first, to see what they could expect. There were doors all the way down to the left. When he peeked to the right, he immediately drew his head back.

"Guards!" he said.

"Standing there in the hallway?" asked Frederick.

Jonah nodded. "Two of them, right in front of a door at the end of the hall."

Eliza smiled, suddenly much more hopeful. "They're guarding him. I know it. That's where he is!"

"Well then, let's go get him!" Andre said, moving through the doorway.

Jonah grabbed his friend's meaty shoulder and pulled him back. "Hold on, Andre. We need some kind of game plan. We can't just barge in."

"Some kind of distraction would be nice," offered Julia. "Something to get them away from the door for a minute, so we can see what's inside?"

"But we need to get in the door, and I'm sure it will be locked," Eliza said. "No doubt those guys have the keys, though."

"You guys create a distraction, and I'll get us those keys," Hai Ling said. Jonah was surprised again at her boldness. She shrugged. "I'm probably the sneakiest one here anyway. Might as well put it to good use."

Hai Ling strode out into the hallway before Jonah or anyone else could protest. She marched down until she was right in front of two guards, standing beside the door. She waved her hand in front of their faces, knowing they couldn't see her, and grinned back down the hallway at the quarterlings.

"I have to hand it to her, she has some guts," Jonah muttered, the others nodding approvingly.

The men were having a discussion about New York City football teams, and which one was better, the New York Jets or the New York Giants. The guard didn't notice when Hai Ling slipped her slender hand into his pocket, pulling out a small ring of keys.

The distraction needed to happen now. Otherwise, the men were going to see a key ring floating in the air beside them.

"Andre, now you can go!"

Andre ran down to the other end of the hallway and shoved a door so hard that it hit the wall behind it, but it stayed open.

"What was that?" one of the guards called out. "Who's there?"

"Go check it out," the other man barked.

Andre stood, waiting, pressed against the wall, as the man hurried down the hallway, hand on his hip, right where his gun was holstered. The man stepped up to the darkened room, peeking in.

"Anyone in here?" he said, flipping on the lights and stepping inside. "Hello?"

When he was all the way in, Andre grabbed the door handle and pulled it shut.

"Okay, guys!" he called out. "I've got him!" Using all his angel strength, he held the doorknob, leaning backward, holding it steady as the man tried to pull it back open.

Jonah could hear his cries from behind the door.

"Help! Hey, Frank, the door's jammed! Help me out here!"

Frank muttered something under his breath and walked down the hall.

"Just turn the knob and open it!" he shouted. "Is that too complicated for a New York Jets fan?"

But when he was almost there, a door beside him flung open.

"Huh?" Frank said, peering into the dark room, and then he stepped inside.

The door suddenly slammed shut behind him.

"Hey! What the . . . ?"

Frederick held on to the knob outside. "I've got this one!" he called out. "You're clear!" The door shook, being beaten on from the other side, but he held on tight. "Move fast, though, okay?"

Jonah, Eliza, and Julia were already down the hallway as Hai Ling worked with the keys to the locked door.

Finally, she found one that fit. "I think this is it!"

She turned the knob and opened the door.

The open door revealed a dark room that was hot and smelled like a gym locker. Jonah fumbled for a light switch along the wall and turned the lights on.

In the far corner of the room, a boy was bound to a metal pole that stretched from the floor to the ceiling. It was Jeremiah.

TWENTY-FIVE

SURPRISE IN THE HALLWAY

Jeremiah!" squealed Eliza, rushing over.

"Yes!" Jonah exclaimed, pumping his fist and joining her.

Jeremiah was squinting up at the lights and sweat was beading on his forehead, but he was there. And alive!

"He can't see us," Jonah said. "We're still in the hidden realm, remember?"

A red glowing strand ran around his head. It was thick enough to cover his mouth.

"What is that around his face?" asked Hai Ling.

Jonah knew. He'd seen it before, years ago. It was the same type of band that the fallen angels had used to hold the nephilim captive.

"It's something the fallen angels put on him," Jonah answered. "Maybe he was talking too much . . ."

He quickly pulled an arrow off his back and held it close to Jeremiah's mouth.

"Wait a minute! Are you sure you know what you're doing?" Hai Ling asked.

"Just please be careful, Jonah," pleaded Eliza.

He rolled his eyes at them both and ran the tip of the arrow along the glowing tendrils until, with a small burst of smoke and light, they fell from Jeremiah's mouth.

Jeremiah looked up, blinking.

"Hey," he said slowly. "I can talk . . . I can actually talk again!"

"I think we should let him see that we're here," Eliza said, smiling. Jonah and Hai Ling nodded, and they bowed their heads and left the hidden realm.

Pop. Pop. Pop.

They appeared instantly in front of Jeremiah.

His mouth dropped open, and he looked at them in disbelief.

"First time I've ever seen you speechless, little bro," Jonah said, grinning. Eliza began to cry, hugging his neck tightly, while Jonah and Hai Ling worked on untying him from the metal pipe.

"You came!" Jeremiah finally said, pulling his arms out of the cords and hugging Eliza, and then Jonah, tightly. Then he gave a big hug to Hai Ling too. "I can't believe you're actually here! I can't believe you found me!"

"I was trying to find Mom when I went back to the warehouse," Jeremiah told them sheepishly. "I was snooping around there, and then the next thing I know, these two big guys grabbed me out on the street and threw me into their car. I tried to fight them, but it was no use."

Jonah smiled, thinking of his brother trying to fight two huge Russian bodyguards. He was sure he had given it his best shot.

"Did you try to use your angelic power?" Eliza asked. "The belt of truth? Or at least just disappear into the hidden realm?"

"Well, I was so scared, I didn't really think about that until they took me to this room," he answered. "I wouldn't have been able to leave the car anyway, even if I was invisible to them. They threw a hood or something over my head, and I couldn't see. When they took it off, I was here. And for some reason, I couldn't talk."

"The fallen angels slapped some kind of binding on your mouth," Jonah said. He looked at Eliza. "I guess they knew about his power."

She thought for a second, nodding slowly. "If they stopped him from talking, they would be able to keep him from speaking truth and using the belt. Brilliant."

"Maybe we can take that mouth covering back with us to use when we need to," said Jonah, laughing.

Eliza rolled her eyes. "Jonah, be serious. We need to get upstairs, and then get off this evil boat before someone notices us. But with you, Frederick, and Andre, and your angelic strength, we should have a pretty good chance."

Hai Ling smirked. "As long as we aren't stopped by any flying bad guys."

"Well, whatever we do, we need to hurry," Jonah said. He could hear Frederick and Andre down the hallway, calling out to them to hurry up. The guards behind the doors were banging louder and louder.

They quickly made their way into the hallway. Andre and Frederick were still holding the doors closed, but they looked relieved to see the group sneaking down the hallway.

Jonah called out instructions as they approached the stairwell. "When I say go, we're going to make a run for it," he said. "You guys get ready, okay?"

Jonah stopped suddenly, motioning for everyone behind him to be quiet.

Someone was walking down the steps.

Clack. Clack. Clack.

He felt a sickness in his stomach grow, and the temperature in the hallway suddenly dropped. He turned to look at Eliza. Her face was pale with fear.

"I don't like this . . . ," she whispered. The others seemed just as rattled.

A man entered the hallway and stood, adjusting the cuff links on his shirt and straightening his tuxedo jacket. He was right in between Jonah's group and Frederick and Andre. Finally, the man looked up, straight into Jonah's eyes, a wide grin on his face.

"I don't see how they wear these things," he said. "But I guess that's the cost of doing business, right?"

He laughed, the only sound in the hallway, except for the two guards still trying to escape the rooms they were trapped in. But as Andre and Frederick turned to see who was in the hallway, they let their grip go, and the doors flung open. The man turned to look at the guards.

"Who's out here?" one of them shouted angrily. "Who's been holding the door?"

When they saw the man in the tuxedo standing there, watching them with a derisive smile on his face, they stood straight up.

"Stuck in a closet, are we, gentlemen?" the man said. "Doesn't appear to be anyone out here except us, does it?"

Frederick and Andre walked toward them, still in the hidden realm and invisible to the guards. They were going to try to sneak around the man.

"Why don't you two go ahead and pop back into reality, huh,

little quarterlings?" he said, still fidgeting with his cuff link. He held his hands out, motioning to the hall. "This is reality, after all, no?" He chuckled again, and Jonah couldn't tell whether he believed that himself or not.

Frederick and Andre looked shocked by his words, realizing he could see them. They glanced at each other, and then silently they both entered the physical world again. They popped into view, and the guards gasped. The man turned back to the other group.

"Nice to see you again, Jonah," he said, moving close to him. He turned to Eliza. "And you too, dear Eliza. What's the matter? You're looking a little pale. Oh well . . . I guess it's not every day you get to be in the presence of someone like me."

The guards looked confused as the man seemed to be talking to invisible people. "Are you all right, Mr. Prince?"

"Why don't you come back into reality too, friends?"

Jonah sighed and nodded to the others, and they popped back into the physical world too.

"Oh, man . . . ," one of the guards said.

Jonah mustered every ounce of courage he had just to speak. "Mr. Prince? Seriously? You can't hide behind that person, whoever you are pretending to be on the outside. We know who you really are."

Mr. Prince smiled at Jonah, taking delight in his words. "Well, I should hope so, Jonah. I've known you practically your entire life."

Jonah bristled. "You don't know me at all."

"Good one, there," Mr. Prince said, pointing at him. "But I know what you were doing while your brother and sister were lost by themselves here in New York. You were showing off on the basketball court, trying to impress all the girls in your school, and forgetting about them. You were taking it easy back in Peacefield."

Eliza glanced at Jonah, and he could sense an invisible wave of her doubt crash over him. He wanted to protest, but instead, he was weighed down by his own crushing feelings.

He's right. I ran away from my family. I ran away from everyone in my life.

"At any rate," the man said, checking his watch, "I have some important people to attend to. But I'd like to continue this conversation later. Wouldn't that be fun?"

He snapped his fingers, and a horde of fallen angels came from the stairwell. Moving quickly, while the quarterlings were still in a daze from their encounter with the Evil One himself, the Fallen grabbed the kids, shoved them to the ground, and pulled their hands behind their backs.

Something felt hot on Jonah's wrists. "Owww!"

He tugged at them but couldn't budge. Even fighting with his angelic strength didn't have any effect. His arms were secured behind his back.

Jonah's face was pressing into the carpet. Out of the corner of his eye he saw Eliza's shoe, squirming and thrashing around.

"Eliza!" he shouted. "Jeremiah! You guys all right?"

The fallen angel on top of him yanked him up.

"Now, don't think we don't know about your other little gift," the fallen one growled. He grabbed Jonah's hip and spun him around, and another red, glowing webbing encircled Jonah's waist. "Wouldn't want you to get any ideas with that fancy angelblade of yours."

All of them were up and on their feet, the quarterlings with their arms bound behind their backs. Jeremiah's mouth was covered again. Eliza's head was even surrounded with a red headband of the same material.

They even know about her helmet of salvation, Jonah thought. He wondered how her practice with it had been going. He'd seen it in action only once, last year at school, and while she was good at using it, it had been a work in progress.

The guards corralled them and forced them into the holding room. Abaddon watched for a few seconds, enjoying the show, but then turned and bounded up the steps. Jonah assumed he was heading to the top deck to enact whatever awful plan he had for some of the world's most important guests. He shuddered to think what he could do if he could control the world's leaders.

Then he remembered—President Kinston was supposed to be there too. This was just getting worse and worse.

The guards and the fallen angels threw them all back in the room. The guards secured the quarterlings to chairs all around the room with ordinary rope and duct tape, and the Fallen wrapped special webbing around them in the hidden realm to keep them from using their gifts. They'd even wrapped up Jonah's, Frederick's, and Hai Ling's feet so that they couldn't use their sandals of speed.

"This ought to take care of you until he gets back," the fallen one securing Jonah's feet growled. "Without your special gifts, you're helpless."

TWENTY-SIX

DISCOVERY

Jonah watched Jeremiah straining against the chair and trying desperately to speak but unable to form any words, only groans and growls in his throat.

"Hey, Jeremiah," Jonah said calmly, "just take it easy. All of that straining isn't going to get you anywhere. I wish you could talk and use your belt of truth to help us get out of here, believe me."

Jeremiah stopped pulling at the post and hung his head, shaking it.

"It's okay," Jonah muttered. "It's not your fault. You saw Mom . . . or at least, thought you saw her. I probably would have done the same thing."

Jeremiah rolled his eyes and glared at him as if to say, *Of course it's my fault . . .*

Hai Ling was right beside Jonah and had begun to whimper, and then shake. "We're in trouble . . . we're in big, big trouble . . . We're stuck in the bottom of a ship, and no one knows we're here.

No one knows we're here!" She was working herself into a panic. Eliza tried to quiet her.

"We're going to figure it out," Julia said hopefully. "We'll make it out of here, Hai Ling. Right, guys?"

Andre shrugged and mumbled something unintelligible.

"Jonah?" Eliza glared at him, looking for an answer. Jonah looked around at all of them, fear growing on their faces by the minute. He tried to think of something, some way to escape. There had to be a way.

He just had no idea what that way was.

"We can't do anything," he finally said to Eliza and Julia with an exasperated sigh. "We're locked in here. How am I supposed to get out an arrow? Or pull out an angelblade? They've got your blade pretty well secured there too. Can you reach yours?" She looked away from him, staring at the ceiling.

Jonah closed his eyes.

What can we do? Think, Jonah. There has to be something, some way out of here. Abaddon's coming back here soon...

Nothing was coming to him, though. He prayed and entered the hidden realm. Maybe there would be something he could see here. Maybe there was something they were missing.

He looked around the room carefully. He could now see the glow of the fingerprint of Elohim on each person there.

A few of his friends were praying, and he could see faint tendrils of light coming from their chests, upward and through the ceiling. He was about to offer up his own prayer when he heard mumbling from his left and realized that Andre was losing it. He was bent over, his head drooping, and he was speaking a stream of unintelligible words.

"Is he praying?" asked Hai Ling, looking at him with her brow wrinkled.

"No, there isn't light coming out of him. I think he's speaking Russian," Jonah said. "Andre, are you all right?"

But he didn't answer Jonah and acted as if he couldn't hear him. He continued speaking in his native tongue, faster and faster. He had begun rocking back and forth.

"I think he's going to explode," Hai Ling observed.

Jonah continued to try to get his attention, along with Jeremiah and Hai Ling. But Andre wouldn't snap out of it.

Eliza, however, was straining to listen and had begun to lean forward as their Russian friend spoke. As she did, a movement caught Jonah's eye. Something was stirring, deep inside her chest. He thought at first she must be praying. It appeared as if the tendrils of light were emerging, and he expected to see them go upward. The thing that confused him, though, was that she didn't appear to be praying. She was listening to Andre speak.

Eliza began to nod, and suddenly her eyes grew bright and her face held an understanding look. "Yes, yes," she was saying as Andre continued to speak.

I'm pretty sure she doesn't speak Russian, unless she learned it when I was gone, Jonah thought. What was just as mesmerizing to him, though, was what was taking place in the hidden realm. The strings of light coming from her were going toward Andre and actually entering his chest, making him glow brighter!

Jonah popped back into the physical world.

"Since when do you know Russian?" Jonah said to her. "You should see what's happening in the hidden realm."

But she held her hand up to him. She was still listening to Andre, nodding her head.

"Since never!" she said, the goofy smile still on her face. "But somehow I can understand every word he's saying."

Before Jonah could even process that, she launched into an energetic response. He couldn't understand a word of it, though, because it was all in Russian. Andre's head snapped up as he heard his language being spoken perfectly by Eliza.

"You haven't learned it, but you can speak it?" Jonah said, but she was too excited to use this newfound gift to hear what he was saying.

The other quarterlings were leaning forward now, having stopped praying to watch the conversation between Andre and Eliza.

"I was in the hidden realm, and something is going on here," Jonah said, pointing to them both.

Frederick raised his eyebrows. "Strands of light, going from her to him?"

Jonah cocked his head. "How did you know?"

"Well," Hai Ling said, "if you'd been with us for the past couple of months, you wouldn't have to ask."

"It's a spiritual gift," said Julia, ignoring Hai Ling's comment and watching Eliza carefully. "She's apparently in the process of discovering a new one. If I'm not mistaken, I'd say it's the gift of tongues."

"Tongues?" Jonah said. "But I thought . . ."

"Amazing!" Eliza and Andre both said at the same time. They were laughing together, and it seemed Andre had snapped out of it.

"I just started to listen to him," Eliza said, "like, really listen, and told myself to try to understand him. Just give it a shot, you know. And all of a sudden, I could hear his words plainly. Like he was just speaking English!"

"Kareem says the gifts can reveal themselves in lots of different ways," answered Hai Ling.

"So you can understand all kinds of different languages?" asked Jonah.

"If she focuses on it, quieting her mind and opening herself up to help another person, then apparently, yes," said Julia.

They each entered the hidden realm now and observed for themselves the light wrapping itself around Andre.

"He was just worried," she said. "I gave him some encouragement and a couple of verses to remember."

"Thanks, Eliza," said Andre, breathing a little easier. "That really helped. I was panicking. But wow, who knew you could speak Russian?"

"I realize that this is great and everything, but it still doesn't help us get out of here," Frederick said.

Jonah shrugged, and then he had a thought. "Maybe there are some other gifts we haven't discovered yet that could help."

They looked at each other, chewing on that for a minute.

"But how do you just discover a new gift?" Andre said. "We never really covered that in class."

"Kareem says it happens through other people around you, observing things," Julia said, "or through prayer ... asking Elohim to reveal them."

The quarterlings studied one another for a minute, but no one had anything constructive to say about gifts they each might possess. Jeremiah looked on too, but of course, he couldn't speak at the moment.

"Maybe we should ask Elohim," Frederick finally said.

They each bowed and focused their thoughts, trying to discover something new about themselves, asking Elohim to reveal their gifts. Jonah closed his eyes and tried to gather all of his thoughts together and point them in this one direction.

But even though he knew he already had the gift of prophecy, all he could see was darkness. Like a blank movie screen in front of him, nothing was playing. It was empty.

He peeked up at the others, who were still hunched over. Andre had his eyes closed tightly. Frederick and Julia were perfectly still. Hai Ling was breathing deeply, settling herself.

Jonah closed his eyes again, and this time, something happened. An image flashed in front of his mind. It was the shadow of a figure walking across the landscape of his thoughts. He couldn't tell who it was, but suddenly, they were holding a flaming sword in their hands, striking it back and forth.

He looked hard, to try to see who it was, but all he could see was shadow.

Jonah opened his eyes. What was he to make of that?

He looked around the room, and the rest were still bowed, except for Hai Ling. She was looking directly at Frederick, her mouth hanging open slightly, as if she wanted to say something but wasn't sure what. She looked dazed.

"Hai Ling?" Jonah said

At the sound of her name, Hai Ling snapped out of it, shuddered, and turned to Jonah. "I have the weirdest feeling."

"What?"

"Frederick has a gift. And he doesn't even know it yet."

Frederick peeked up at them with one eye. "What did you say? You think I have a gift? Because I'm trying here, but I'm not seeing anything about any new gift."

Jonah thought about his own vision. *Could it be about Frederick?*

"It sounds to me like you are experiencing some deeper level of discernment," Eliza said. "Which is a spiritual gift of its own. That's what you're doing, right? You have this deep feeling?"

Hai Ling nodded, biting her lip and barely keeping herself together.

"Well, let's throw this into the mix," said Jonah. "I just saw a shadowy figure with a sword . . ."

"And you do have the gift of prophecy!" Eliza said, snapping her fingers. "Frederick?"

He looked at them, bewildered. "I don't have an angelblade, if that's what you're after," he said rather sullenly. "Believe me, I've tried. I just don't have it."

"Try again," urged Eliza. "You never know when Elohim wants to reveal His gifts. I'm a great example of that."

The ropes the guards had used on Frederick wrapped around his chest. His arms were secured behind his back, but not to the chair itself. "Give me a minute," he said.

He pulled his legs up as high as he could, and with a great amount of contortion, forced his hands down from behind his back, to behind his legs, then finally underneath his feet. They were still bound together by the red glowing chains, but they were now in front of him.

Frederick looked at Jonah briefly, raising his eyebrows.

"Just reach to your hip and pull," Jonah said.

Frederick tugged both of his hands to his left hip and made a dragging motion quickly. To all of their surprise, a flaming sword lit the room.

225

TWENTY-SEVEN

AT THE BOTTOM
OF THE POOL

It was a deep shade of red, and the glow from the blade lit their faces. The other quarterlings were in awe, marveling at the discovery. Frederick couldn't help but break into a full-fledged grin, waving his new weapon in the air and testing its weight.

"I never thought I'd actually get one of these," he said, holding it up in front of his face. "It feels different than I imagined it would."

"Hey, it's cool and all that," Jonah said, holding up his feet, "but how about you put that blade to work?"

"Oh," Frederick said, finally snapping his eyes away from the blade, "right. Reach out."

Jonah held his feet up. "Careful, now."

"Is it sharp?" asked Frederick as he slowly maneuvered the blade above Jonah's ankles.

Jonah wrinkled his forehead. "Really, Frederick? It'll take two seconds for that thing to cut my feet off! Steady yourself."

Frederick lightly touched the blade against the chains holding Jonah's feet, and they fell to the ground and fizzled away into nothing. Jonah was then able to push himself up and spin around enough for Frederick to free his hands from behind the chair.

Jonah pulled out his own blade. "Let me return the favor," he said, quickly slicing through Frederick's chains, freeing up his hands.

They made quick work of the rest of the chains, and then ropes, until everyone was standing up and rubbing their wrists.

"What about the guards?" Julia asked.

Andre was holding up the rope. "I would say we have everything we need to take care of them right here."

Jonah glanced at Frederick, who nodded, putting his angel-blade away. He then knocked on the door and waited.

The guards quickly opened the door, obviously surprised to hear someone knocking when they were all supposed to be tied down.

"Hi," Jonah said, waving to the confused men. The guards stormed into the room and reached for Jonah. Jonah took a step back, though, and Andre and Frederick jumped on both of them. They both easily pinned the men down with their angelic strength.

Julia, Eliza, and Hai Ling wrapped the guards' hands and feet with the rope as fast as they could. Soon the two guards were incapacitated.

"You can't do this to us!" one of the men shouted. "You're gonna regret it!"

Jonah smiled, holding up two long pieces of duct tape.

"Actually, we *can* do this to you, and I don't think we'll regret it at all. You're awfully loud, anyway."

He wrapped the tape around their mouths, and they could only look at him wide-eyed, groaning as they flailed around on the floor.

"Be as quiet as you can," Eliza reminded her friends as they gathered by the door.

Hai Ling nodded. "We know, we know. Let's just get out of here, okay?"

They filed out of the room, tiptoeing along the carpeted floor until they came to the stairwell. One flight up, and they were back to the pool level. No one was around. Jonah was sure all of the workers were upstairs, attending to the guests.

They were almost to the door of the next set of steps when Jonah heard a splash in the pool. Just a small slap on top of the water, like a kid would make playing in the summertime. He turned toward the pool and saw a small ripple in the center, moving outward toward the edges.

"What are you looking at, Jonah?" Eliza said, noticing him staring. "We need to—"

A high-pitched scream pierced the air. Before Jonah knew it, Julia had fallen down and was being dragged along the ground toward the pool.

A green tentacle was wrapped around her foot and was pulling her toward whatever was in the water.

Jeremiah dove for her hands and caught one of them, slowing down her slide across the floor for a second.

"I've got you, Julia! Hold on!" he said. But he began to get pulled too. Hai Ling and Frederick grabbed him by the feet, and all of a sudden it was a tug-of-war, with Jeremiah and Julia stuck in the middle.

"You're going to pull them in half!" Eliza shouted.

Jonah pulled out his angelblade, heading for the edge of the pool. He could see a dark, shapeless form of a creature under the water. There were two others beside it.

Jonah was mid-swing with his sword when he felt himself lurch backward. The sword met only air, and he was suddenly dangling above the water. Another tentacle had wrapped itself around his chest and was squeezing tightly.

The pressure forced Jonah's hand loose, and his angelblade hit the water with a loud splash.

The monster holding him emerged from the water, and he realized that it wasn't a tentacle holding him—it was a tail. An enormous, winged snake was glaring at him with beady eyes as water from its wings rained down below.

"Aaaaahhh!" he yelled. But halfway through his scream, he got a mouthful of water. The creature had yanked him down into the pool.

The water wasn't deep, and he was tall, but he soon realized that didn't matter if he couldn't stand up. And right now, the creature was squeezing even harder and holding him under.

Jonah pulled against the tail, trying to tear into the flesh of the creature and free himself. But nothing was working. The snake-like creature was too strong, even though he was fighting against it with all of the angel strength he had.

He heard another splash beside him and saw Eliza, her face twisted in terror, pulling against another tail. Then yet another body entered the pool, wrapped in a tentacle. It was Jeremiah.

This made Jonah fight even harder, and he was able to push the tail away from him for a brief second. He spotted his angelblade, a few feet away from him on the pool bottom. If he could just get enough room to get his arm free and reach down . . .

Snap! The snake tail clamped down around him again. Jonah was starting to feel dizzy. He needed air soon. His thoughts were getting cloudy, and he felt himself growing weaker.

His mind wandered. His dad, Benjamin, came into his thoughts, walking toward him through a fog. He missed his dad. Jonah had been so mad, and he'd let his father bear the brunt of it. But Jonah loved him, and he felt his heart breaking, knowing that he wouldn't get to see his dad ever again. Everything was fading, darkness moving in from the corner of his vision, until all he could see was a circle, a tunnel of light . . .

His mother was there now. Eleanor Stone, right in front of him, so close he could have reached out and touched her if his arms were free.

"Mom?"

"Jonah," she said, smiling, her green eyes dancing in front of him, bright, as if they'd just seen a million stars. "I love you so much. Always know that."

"I do, Mom," he said, "I know. I love you too. I miss you so much. I can't . . . I can't do this without you here. I've messed everything up . . ."

Her eyes were filled with love, more than he could ever imagine. "It's okay, son. Elohim loves you very much." When she said the words, he felt that love, cascading over his heart. "I can't wait for you to see it here, Jonah. It's beautiful. Indescribable. You have to see it to believe it. But for now," she said, rubbing his face with her hand, "you have more to do. More life to live, more purpose to fulfill. We'll see each other again soon."

A flash of red light snapped Jonah out of his haze, causing him to look to his right. When he looked back, she was gone.

But he felt the tail loosen, and then completely fall off. His feet hit the pool floor, and he stood up, his head finally above water. He sucked in the air his lungs so desperately needed.

Frederick was swinging his blade down close to Eliza now, and then Jeremiah, freeing them both with a swipe of his sword. The severed tails floated to the surface of the water, coloring the pool water with a dark green liquid.

The creatures were thrashing in the pool, either in pain or angry. Their forked tongues were sliding in and out of their mouths, hissing.

Jonah spotted his blade again and dove down to grab it. He reemerged and swam to his brother and sister.

Eliza was free and making a straight line for the side of the pool. Jeremiah was right behind her, coughing and choking, but pushing himself through the water.

"Were those snakes? They had wings!" asked Eliza as they all pulled themselves out of the pool. She continued to babble breathlessly. "The prophet Isaiah talked about fiery serpents coming from the desert ..."

"Frederick!" Jonah called out, ignoring her. Frederick was still in the pool, holding his blade in between him and the creatures, who were injured but not done fighting.

"I've got this, just get out of here!" Frederick shouted, training his eyes on the creatures. Their eyes were only slits, sitting toward the back of their long, narrow heads.

"Frederick, we have to make a run for it!" Jonah cried. "Now!"

Frederick heard that and took a step back, still holding his sword, but looking a little less confident. "Just get up the steps!"

But Jonah couldn't just leave him. He'd spent too long leaving everyone already. He was done with that.

"Eliza?" Jonah turned to her, and she nodded, already knowing what he was thinking.

"Just go help him!" she said.

Andre and Hai Ling had a protesting Jeremiah and were already heading up the steps.

"You're coming with me now, and that's the end of the discussion!" Jonah heard Eliza say to Jeremiah just before Jonah dove back into the pool.

He stood beside Frederick, swords raised side by side. "Did you hear me?" Jonah said. "These things are under Abaddon's control. Might be time to get out of here."

The creatures lashed out, and the two boys ducked.

"Come on!" Frederick yelled at the creatures. He looked so enraged that Jonah thought he might charge the beasts. He grabbed Frederick by the shoulder, pulling him backward.

The flying serpents swung again, but this time, both boys were ready. Slicing their blades through the air, they hacked at the creature's tails, filling the pool with gore.

The creatures roared, thrashing around violently.

"Nice!" Jonah shouted. "Now, come on!"

Frederick and Jonah backed up to the edge of the pool, hauled themselves out, and then ran for the exit.

TWENTY-EIGHT

PARTY ON THE DECK

As they ran up the steps to catch up with the others, Frederick shoved his sword back beside his hip, and it disappeared.

"Looks like you're going to enjoy that," Jonah said.

Frederick couldn't help but smile. "Yeah, thanks. That was fun . . . in a weird kind of way."

Jonah slapped him on the back as they found the main level and rounded the corner.

The rest of the quarterlings were gathered around the exit door that would lead down the ramp, onto the dock, and hopefully into the safety of darkness.

Andre was looking through the round window at the exit door. "There're still two guards down there, guys. At the bottom of the ramp."

Jeremiah put his hand on the door. "I know how to take care of them," he said. "Come on, just disappear with me for a second."

Andre and Jeremiah entered the hidden realm, opened the door, and began to walk down the ramp.

The men turned toward the boat, seeing the door open. "Is someone up there?" one of them shouted.

"Maybe the wind blew it open," the other one suggested. "We should go check it out, I guess."

By the time the guards started up the ramp, Andre and Jeremiah were already there. They reentered the visible world right in front of the guards.

"Boo!" Jeremiah shouted, right in their faces.

The guards' mouths dropped open, but before they had a chance to react, Andre gave them both a hard shove off the ramp.

"Aaaahhhhh!" the guards shouted as they fell backward off the dock and down into the murky water below. There weren't any ladders nearby, so the quarterlings had a few minutes to escape before the guards got out of the water.

"Okay, let's go!" Eliza said as Andre and Jeremiah waved them down urgently. Eliza, Hai Ling, and Julia sprinted down the ramp, single file.

Jonah and Frederick both made their way down backward, looking out for anyone who might be chasing them.

"Maybe we're going to get lucky," Frederick said. There were no fallen angels up above. At least, none they could see in the black darkness of the night.

Jonah nodded, keeping his eyes trained above.

He could only imagine what the fallen angels who were guarding the yacht were doing. The faces of the guests he'd stood in line with crossed his mind. They had no idea what kind of trap they were walking into. He was sure they'd never experienced the level of evil they were about to face.

Jonah wondered if the president of the United States had made it. Glancing over at the street, he saw five sleek, black sport utility vehicles parked one behind the other, each flying small American flags from the hood. He had his answer.

"Guys," he called out, but they didn't seem to hear him. "Guys!" The rest of them stopped, turning to look back at him.

"Come on, Jonah!" Eliza said urgently. "Why are you stopping?"

He pointed to the armored vehicles. "We need to go back."

Eliza glared at him and put her hand on Jeremiah's shoulder. "Seriously? We have what we came for."

Jonah shook his head. "You know what's up there as well as I do . . ."

"So we'll alert the angels," said Eliza. "We'll tell them to bring everyone they have. There's no reason you should put yourself—"

"Eliza!" he said. Then he took a breath and quieted his voice. "Someone needs to go up there now. Abaddon and his creeps are up there with the president of the United States and a bunch of other important people. Don't you think something needs to be done?"

She didn't answer, and he knew he'd won. "You don't have to come, but I'm going."

Jonah turned back toward the ship. But immediately he knew he wasn't alone. He turned around to find Andre and Frederick walking behind him, with Jeremiah, Julia, Hai Ling, and Eliza bringing up the rear.

"You're not going back up there on your own," said Frederick. He was looking at Jonah as if he were daring him to disagree. "I'll come with you."

Jonah nodded, but then looked at his little brother. "Well, you're definitely not coming!"

Jeremiah kept walking. "You left us for a year. You don't get to tell me what to do anymore."

Jonah started to protest, but he dropped it. What could he say to that?

As they walked quickly back, Jonah was hoping to see a massive group of angels soaring over their heads, but the sky remained frustratingly empty.

"I guess the angels don't know what's going on here yet," he said.

Frederick grinned. "Well, they'll get to hear all about the fight they missed when we get back."

Jeremiah smiled and high-fived Frederick, but Jonah was a little worried that Frederick's new weapon was already going to his head.

They reentered the hidden realm just before they came to the pier. The guards were standing at the bottom of the ramp again, this time flanked by four additional men. The two were soaking wet, standing in their suits, and still looked horribly confused.

"I don't think those guys knew what hit them," said Jonah, laughing a little in spite of the dangerous situation.

"We have to move fast," said Frederick, stepping out in front to lead the charge.

They maneuvered around the group of guards, who were having a heated conversation about what was happening on the boat. Two more men came running down the ramp at full speed.

"They're gone! They're gone!"

Jonah knew exactly who the guard was talking about, and they watched the men run down the pier.

Jonah shot off a quick prayer to Elohim for their safety. They would need His help and protection in order to make it back through the boat.

Elohim, please be with us! Keep us safe and help us do what we need to do!

As they headed up the ramp, Jonah spotted a fluttering overhead and stopped in his tracks.

"Up there." He pointed. "Did you guys see something?"

They craned their necks upward. Something was up there, flying in circles over the boat.

"They don't exactly look like any fallen angels I've seen," Julia said.

Jonah frowned. "Griffins again. It's just more of them than I've ever seen before."

This caused all of them to pause, except for Frederick, who reached for his angelblade. Jonah quickly grabbed his hand. "Not yet, Frederick. We don't want them to see your bright new toy and let them know we're here yet, do we?"

Frederick contemplated this, then nodded, pulling his hand away.

Thankfully, the men rushing out had left the door ajar, so they made it back inside without having to create any more unnecessary movement. There were more men coming down the steps in front of them, though, and Jonah, Jeremiah, and Frederick stepped to the side. These were dressed differently than the others, with dark suits and earpieces in their ears.

"Secret service," Jonah whispered. Jeremiah beamed at them, and Jonah gave him a stern look. "Don't get any ideas and don't get distracted, Jeremiah. Our job is upstairs."

They moved quickly up to the next level and then into the circular staircase, which would lead them to the top deck.

"Okay, now's a good time for those blades," he said to Frederick and Eliza, pulling his own angelblade out. Jonah turned to the others. "And you get ready with your weapons too. Since we don't really know what we're facing, we'll need all the help we can get."

They peered around the open doorway at the top of the stairs at the party in full swing.

"Whoa," Jeremiah said.

"Yeah," answered Jonah.

There was a tall metal heater beside them, pumping out heat into the cold air. A dozen or more of the same were placed around the deck to make it feel as if it were summer, even though winter had officially begun. People in tuxedos and fancy dresses were everywhere, sipping out of tall, thin glasses and plucking hors d'oeuvres from silver trays carried by solemn waiters. A string orchestra was playing softly in the corner.

"Oh man, that's President Kinston!" shouted Jeremiah, pointing. "I've seen him on TV a million times!"

"Be quiet!" Eliza said, glancing around, not wanting to be heard by anyone in the hidden realm. But they were all mesmerized for a few seconds by the sight of the president himself, standing with a group of people who were all laughing at something he'd said.

Jonah drew in a sharp breath. Standing right next to the president was Abaddon, a.k.a. Mr. Prince. Touching the elbow of the president of the United States, Abaddon leaned over and whispered something into his ear. The president nodded and smiled.

Jonah felt his stomach churn, and for a moment he thought he might be sick. But why would he expect anything less? If the fallen angels were targeting places like Peacefield High School, of course they were trying to attack the most powerful person in the world. And the Evil One himself was right in the middle of it.

Seeing him made Jonah want to do one of two things—run and hide, or charge ahead with his sword raised and all the strength he had. Being with his friends gave him courage, and he raised his sword and inched forward, ready to make a move. But Abaddon made a move first.

"Ladies and gentlemen," Mr. Prince said in a loud voice, moving to the back end of the deck. He stood up on a platform that held the orchestra so that his head rose above the crowd. Jonah felt Mr. Prince's gaze fall on him for a second.

I'm glad you're here to see this, Jonah . . .

The voice snaked into his mind like frozen rain, icing everything it touched.

The man shot his eyes upward for the smallest second, and Jonah saw the creatures, who had been circling high above, begin to move downward.

"I asked the ambassador if I could say a few words to you all on this special occasion," he began. Jonah saw the Russian ambassador standing off to the side, a glazed look on his face.

Abaddon has him totally under his control, Jonah thought. He wondered how long it would take to have the president, and the rest of these people, responding to his every desire too. And what would that mean? Could governments fall under his control? Armies? Entire countries?

Jonah knew that that was exactly what the Evil One wanted— to tear out hearts and to rip lives away from God. He wanted to take people with him to a place of hatred, hopelessness, and despair, far away from anything good.

Mr. Prince continued talking, but Jonah wasn't listening to him anymore.

There was activity in the sky in every direction. The griffins had been joined by fallen angels, and they were all hovering above the guests waiting for some sort of cue from Abaddon.

"Looks like everyone's been invited to the party," Jonah said.

As Abaddon made a sweeping gesture with his arms, the griffins attacked. They swooped down and dug into the guests, none of whom offered any resistance.

He wondered if something in Abaddon's voice had caused the people to glaze over, just like the Russian ambassador, turning them into easy, unsuspecting targets for the claws of the griffins.

The first one down landed on the shoulders of President Kinston himself, sinking its claws deeply into his back.

"It's now or it's never, guys!" Jonah said, and he charged ahead.

The griffins weren't expecting the attack, and the first one he came to was clawing at an older woman in a sparkly gown.

"Get off her, you freak!" he shouted, swinging the shining silver blade right through its midsection. The beast fell to the ground before it could even make a sound.

He swung at the next one he came to with the same result. Glancing quickly to his left, he saw a flash of dark red and knew Frederick had followed his lead. Eliza was swinging her blade furiously too.

Behind him, Jonah heard the high, strong voice of his brother, speaking words of truth: "None of you have any power at all compared to Elohim Himself!"

A flash of light came from Jeremiah's waist, and another griffin went down.

Of course, by now they had most certainly been spotted by the fallen angels, and Jonah was sure the battle was about to get much tougher.

He pushed himself to move faster, and he narrowly avoided getting caught in one of the creature's claws. Spinning back and swinging, Jonah caught it off guard and sent it to the ground. The second one had its claws outstretched, reaching for the back of his neck, when it was blasted out of the way by a burst of light.

Jonah turned to see Jeremiah, who grinned and gave him a small wave. Jonah gave him a thumbs-up and headed for the next griffin.

Jonah was trying to keep an eye on the president, but so much was going on around him he kept losing sight of him. Another griffin was to his left, attacking the man who had stood behind him in line. He was listening to Abaddon talk, but with eyes that looked empty and cold. The griffin had already dug deep inside of him and pulled out a glowing orb of light.

It held the man's heart and soul in its claw.

It was about to rip it away when Jonah met its leg with his blade, severing it completely. It let go of its prize, and the light slid back inside the man's chest as the griffin fell to the floor.

Jonah spotted the president again. An enormous creature was sitting on his back and held the president's light in its talons, toying with it. Mr. Prince was still talking calmly, but Jonah knew he was secretly gloating at the scene unfolding before him. As Jonah watched, he could see the real Abaddon underneath the Mr. Prince facade. Soon, the slick man in the expensive suit was replaced by a hunched figure in a hooded cloak with long, greasy hair and bony fingers.

Abaddon moved toward the president and reached for his exposed soul, clutched by the griffin.

Jonah quickly sheathed his sword and, in one motion, pulled an arrow off his back, produced the bow, and fired.

The white-flamed arrow zipped through the air, tearing through the skull of the griffin. The creature fell to the ground, and the president's light slipped back into his body.

Abaddon turned and stared at Jonah for a few seconds, his cheek twitching. He felt the Evil One's hatred pour over him, and he wanted to look away, but he couldn't. Suddenly, he felt massive arms grab his and pull them behind him. He strained against them with everything he had, but a large, muscular fallen angel was holding him very tightly.

Abaddon strode over to him, snapping back his hood. His glare seemed to dig down into Jonah's very soul. Jonah couldn't look away.

"Jonah, didn't I tell you to wait downstairs?" Abaddon cooed as he walked toward him. "You're always so good at interrupting things. It's been quite frustrating. But not this time."

Jonah trembled, but he called up all the strength and courage he had left. "I don't care what you do to me. But you're not going to get away with this. You can't expect to just . . . take all these people's souls."

Abaddon gestured to the assembled crowd, all passively allowing the griffins to do their work. "Look how they're eating out of my hand, Jonah Stone. They can't help it. It must be something about the sound of my voice . . ." He chuckled to himself.

"You're tricking them," Jonah said. "They don't really love you. They don't want to give you their souls. You're forcing them to do it."

Abaddon raised his arms, shrugging his shoulders. "They're letting themselves be taken, Jonah. I couldn't do this if they didn't want me to. Don't you see? They're all going to be mine. And there is little you and your friends can do to stop it. In fact, while we're at it . . ."

He beckoned to the sky. A griffin, who had been hovering over them, landed on Jonah's back.

Jonah thrashed backward and screamed up toward the night

sky. The pain seared through his chest, and he felt intense heat shoot from the center of his body out into his fingertips and toes. The creature's claws were digging in, searching, prying things loose, going farther and farther.

Finally, the griffin pulled out something glowing and bright, still attached to his chest by strands of light.

Abaddon's eyes narrowed as he looked down at Jonah's soul. "These ancient creatures are marvelous, aren't they, Jonah? They have this amazing ability to identify the heart and soul in anyone. Of course, I taught them to pick it apart from everything else and extract it. May I?"

Jonah didn't know why he asked for permission because he didn't wait for an answer. He simply reached out and grabbed the ball of light, holding it in his hands.

Jonah felt himself begin to slip away. What was he thinking? Why had he put everyone in danger to come back? There was no way they were ever going to come out of this alive. He had known that in the back of his head, and now they were all going to pay for it.

Now the Evil One held his very soul in his grip. He was staring at it, rolling it over in his hands, and studying it.

"You know what I see here, Jonah?" he asked. He waited for a few seconds, but Jonah was growing too weak to respond. "I'll tell you. I see someone with so much evil in them that I honestly don't know how you've made it this far in the first place. Your grandfather, after all, was one of them!" He pointed behind Jonah, to the fallen angel holding him. He and the creature began to laugh. "I mean, seriously, how could you expect to follow Elohim at all? You've always known that evil was going to take over one of these days, haven't you? You can't resist it . . ."

Maybe he was right. Jonah had tried to follow Elohim so

many times, and it always seemed like he failed. No matter what he did, it was never enough. The thought hit him, crashed over him and then crushed him: Abaddon was right. Jonah was evil. He was born that way—evil fallen angel blood literally coursed through his veins. He was doomed.

Jonah felt himself slipping . . .

"That's right, let go," he was saying. "I'll take care of the rest. Leave Elohim in the past. Let Him go, leave Him behind, and come with me . . ."

Just then, a blaring sound rocked through the upper deck of the ship, and Jonah's eyes snapped open again. What was that noise? It sounded distant at first but quickly grew louder.

Abaddon let go of Jonah's soul.

Red lights began flashing on the deck, and people began to rush toward the exit. It was a fire alarm.

The Evil One turned toward the president. "No," he said, looking around frantically. The Secret Service were huddling around the president, ushering him away.

"No, no, no!" Abaddon said. He turned from Jonah and tried to regain control of his party.

Jonah didn't waste any time finding his friends. Frederick was in the corner, pushing himself up from the ground, a griffin flying away from him. Eliza was on the other side, doing the same thing. Julia and Hai Ling were crouching under her shield of faith but seemed to be safe.

Eliza looked weak and pale, but she spoke with a clear voice. "He was holding my soul, right in his claws."

Jonah scanned the deck quickly. He knew they all needed to get away as fast as they could. "Where's Jeremiah? Did anyone see him? He's not up here anywhere."

Frederick shook his head as he slowly pushed himself to his feet. "I don't know. I'm sorry. I was having enough of a time with these awful beasts."

Eliza sprang up. "He's gone *again*?"

Jonah ran down the steps, pushing himself through person after person, who all screamed from the shock of the contact with him in the hidden realm, but he didn't care. He wasn't going to lose his brother twice.

In seconds, he was on the main level. People were milling about, and he saw the back of the president's head as he was thrust through the opening of the yacht and down the ramp.

"Jeremiah!" he called out. "Jeremiah!"

Then Jonah spotted him. Jeremiah was standing next to the flashing light of the fire alarm, which had been broken into and yanked down.

Jonah ran over and wrapped his arms around his brother, hugging him as tightly as he'd ever held anybody.

"Do you think Eliza will be mad that I pulled the fire alarm?" Jeremiah said, pushing back from his brother.

Jonah batted him on the back of the head. "You saved everybody, Jeremiah. I think this time she'll be just fine."

Eliza came running up behind them. "That was you?" she said, pulling him into a hug. "Good job, Jeremiah!"

"My children, it's so great to see how much you love each other."

They all spun, each one recognizing the voice of the person walking down the staircase. She was a tall, slender woman with her hair pulled back in a ponytail—Eleanor Stone.

In spite of what he knew to be true, Jonah's heart leaped.

"Mom!" Jeremiah ran toward her before Eliza or Jonah could grab him and pull him back.

Eleanor leaned down and embraced her son, looking at Jonah and Eliza as she held Jeremiah tightly.

"No hugs from you two?" she said, still smiling. "I understand. I'm sure it is quite strange to see me here. But I'm here. I'm alive! It was all a hoax. Isn't that wonderful?"

Jonah shook his head. His eyes had to be playing tricks on him. He had seen her die. But maybe . . . he wanted to believe she was really alive so badly.

Her body hadn't actually been recovered . . .

His mind was turning somersaults, trying to figure out a way that it was possible. He felt his feet slowly begin to slide toward her. She was holding Jeremiah tightly, reaching out with her other arm to beckon him forward. Her voice was so soothing. In the last year, he'd heard it only in his dreams.

Eliza's voice, though, brought him back to reality.

"If you're our mom, tell me this—what animal did I play in my second-grade musical?" she asked.

Eleanor laughed. "What kind of silly question is that? Come here, dear. I want to see you up close too."

Jonah stopped, steeled by his sister's question. "I think you should answer it."

She gave him a pitiful, pleading look. "Just to make sure," he stammered.

Eleanor let Jeremiah go and placed her hands on her hips. Her smile was fading. "Nonsense. How could you not believe that this is me? Come, feel my skin and touch my arm if you don't believe me."

"Just . . . answer . . . the . . . question!" Eliza said, fuming.

Eleanor suddenly snatched Jeremiah toward her forcefully.

"Hey!" he said, squirming, but he couldn't release himself from her grip.

"I just can't believe that my own children would doubt that I'm really here, right now," she said. But she began to pull Jeremiah backward with her, inching toward the steps again.

Jonah silently prayed, *Elohim, give me wisdom.*

She took one more step backward. Another and she would be on the steps going upward. Jeremiah was still pulling at her arm, which was locked around his shoulders.

In one swift motion, Jonah pulled an arrow from his back, strung it, and fired.

His aim was true. It hit her right in the forehead.

Eleanor's grip loosened, and Jeremiah yanked himself away and ran to Eliza. The woman who look liked their mother morphed into a dark fallen angel. She screamed for a moment as she disintegrated, and then she was gone.

EPILOGUE

Jonah, Eliza, and Jeremiah walked across the field toward their father. He waved to them from a distance and then turned to continue talking with the group of people beside him.

"So you're really back, Jonah?" Jeremiah asked.

"I'm back," Jonah said, trying to be as patient as he could with the question he'd heard for at least the hundredth time from his brother, sister, father, and friends. He knew they'd probably need to hear his answer more than once, though, before they really would believe him. "I'm done running, or at least I hope I am. I guess in a way, I don't regret it, because my journey brought me back to you guys at just the right time. That's the way Elohim is. But I don't plan to ever leave you again."

There wasn't an hour that passed that he didn't think about being trapped in that bus, alone and in the dark, and then turning back to Elohim, feeling His love and forgiveness once again.

He didn't ever want to lose that feeling.

Jeremiah began to run toward their dad, who grabbed his son and swung him around and around.

"I think Dad's doing well," Eliza said, looking back up at Jonah.

He nodded, smiling. "I think we're all doing pretty well, E."

They stepped up to the outside of the small circle of people. Benjamin was talking to them earnestly.

"Jonah brought to my attention the darkness hovering over this place," he said, pointing his thumb over his shoulder to the building. "So I thought it would be a good idea if we held a prayer walk here today. It's a chance for us to join Elohim in the battle for the hearts, minds, and souls of the precious kids who attend Peacefield High. Are you with me?"

He grinned as the members of his congregation cheered.

"Well then, let's get started!"

"Dad, I need to go to the bathroom. I'll be back soon," said Jonah.

"Me too!" said Jeremiah.

Eliza shrugged, smiling slyly at her father. "I guess I'll head that way too and keep an eye on these guys."

As the three rounded the back corner of the school building, they silently prayed, entering the hidden realm.

"Nice of you to join us," a voice called out.

Frederick was standing ahead, smiling broadly, with his angel-blade raised. David, Julia, and the rest of the quarterlings stood beside him.

"I was thinking the same thing," came a voice from above. It was Henry, their old guardian angel, who was waiting with a squadron of warrior angels, hard-nosed and ready for battle.

"Henry!" Jeremiah said, high-fiving his angel friend.

"It's about time you guys showed up," said Eliza, but even she couldn't help but crack a smile.

Jonah clapped his hands. "All right, my dad has the prayer team surrounding this building. What do you say we head inside and see what kind of bad guys we can find?"

"We'll see you inside then," Henry said, signaling to the angels, who snapped their wings and zoomed up the side of the building and out of sight.

Jonah pulled out his angelblade and led the quarterlings through an open door in the side of the building.

As they entered, white tendrils of light were beginning to form around the school from those lifting up the school's students and teachers, declaring the love of Elohim to them and to the heavens.

ACKNOWLEDGMENTS

Writing a novel is so much fun! And so much work... work that wouldn't happen without the support, help, and love of a bunch of people who deserve a shout out.

My kids, Christopher, Luke, and Bailey, are the reason I write, and never far from my thoughts when I work. I'm grateful to be a part of their lives, for their enthusiasm and excitement for these books, and that they get to play a huge role in them. It is one of the great privileges of my life to be your dad.

Thanks to my parents, Charles and Camilla, who continue to shower me with unconditional love and support. These pages would never have seen the light of day without you. Thank you for raising me to always seek the truth.

To my fantastic editor Molly Hodgin, and the entire Thomas Nelson team, thank you for your inspired efforts, insightful critique, constant encouragement, and vision for this project. I'm incredibly blessed and grateful to have partners like you, who care about kids and want to see them grow in their relationship with God. You guys rock!

To my agent, Amanda Luedeke, and the great people at MacGregor Literary, thank you for your wisdom and valuable insight. I'm looking forward to the journey ahead!

As for the readers who have found their way to the Jonah Stone: Son of Angels series . . . I'm beyond thrilled to be able to share these stories with you! You are always on my mind as I write, I have prayed for you, and I hope that your view of God is strengthened, encouraged, and challenged through this book. And I hope this was as fun for you to read as it was for me to write. I can't wait to share another story with you soon.

And Jesus, the simple, profound truth is this . . . I owe You everything.

ABOUT THE AUTHOR

Jerel Law is a gifted communicator and pastor with twenty years of full-time ministry experience. He holds a master of divinity degree from Gordon-Conwell Theological Seminary and began writing fiction as a way to encourage his children's faith to come alive. Law lives in North Carolina with his family. Learn more at www.jerellaw.com.

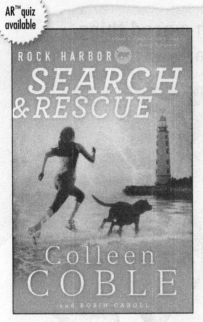

FROM AWARD-WINNING AUTHOR COLLEEN COBLE COMES HER FIRST SERIES FOR YOUNG ADVENTURERS: A MIXTURE OF MYSTERY, SUSPENSE, ACTION—AND ADORABLE PUPPIES!

Eighth-grader Emily O'Reilly is obsessed with all things Search-and-Rescue. The almost-fourteen-year-old spends every spare moment on rescues with her stepmom Naomi and her canine partner Charley. But when an expensive necklace from a renowned jewelry artist is stolen under her care at the fall festival, Emily is determined to prove her innocence to a town that has immediately labeled her guilty.

As Emily sets out to restore her reputation, she isn't prepared for the surprises she and the Search-and-Rescue dogs uncover along the way. Will Emily ever find the real thief?

BY COLLEEN COBLE

www.tommynelson.com

www.colleencoble.com